SEA FEVER

SEA FEVER

K. M. Peyton

Illustrated by Victor G. Ambrus

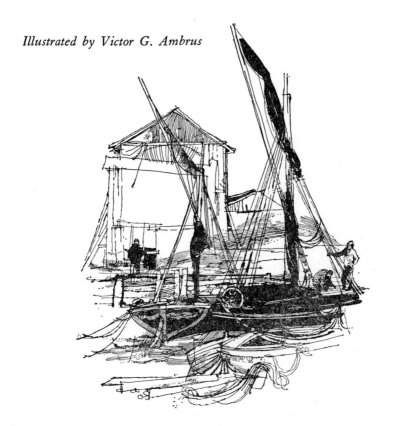

THE WORLD PUBLISHING COMPANY
CLEVELAND AND NEW YORK

Published by The World Publishing Company
2231 West 110th Street, Cleveland 2, Ohio
Published simultaneously in Canada by
Nelson, Foster & Scott Ltd.
Library of Congress Catalog Card Number: 63-18464

First American Edition 1963
Published in England under the title *Windfall*

wp863

To my mother

CONTENTS

The Invitation   9

The *Good Fortune*   22

The Wreck of the *Seaflower*   36

Tom Pullen's Jibe   57

The Money Belt   67

Uncle Albert Calls   76

A Schooner in the Fog   93

A Hand for the *Good Fortune*   113

The Skipper   121

Beckett's Threat   136

The Eve of the Regatta   155

Good Fortune's Race   169

Fathom's Last Sail   182

Matt Goes Home   195

The *Rose in June*   209

Beckett   225

The Invitation

Matt Pullen yawned as he stood beside his father at the tiller. The breeze was cold now, pushing *Fathom*'s patched old sails against the dour evening sky, and the first lights shining on shore were bright with the promise of a hot supper, a good fire, and blessed sleep.

"A good day, eh, lad?"

His father was looking pleased with himself, as always when *Fathom* with a good catch aboard was out on her own. The rest of the fishing smacks straggled way behind, fanned out over a wide area. Only one was within hailing distance and that was *Charity*, Beckett's new cutter. Tom Pullen liked

9

to beat the others, and when a smart-looking craft like *Charity* couldn't pull up with him Tom's day was made.

"Ha, old Beckett will be cursing us, I'll swear," he chuckled. "And to think my old *Fathom*'d passed her half century before *Charity* there was put on the stocks for building!"

"Aye."

Fathom was old, it was true (she had been built for Matt's grandfather in 1825), but Matt couldn't help wondering if it was anything to boast about. He liked the look of *Charity*'s new sails, blood-red against the metallic sky. They wouldn't blow to ribbons if a squall came up unexpectedly. *Fathom*'s canvas, on the other hand, averaged one new patch a week. He looked astern over their marbled wake with slightly envious eyes.

"I like *Charity*," he said. "But I don't like Beckett," he added as an afterthought.

Matt, Pullen's eldest son, had worked on his father's smack ever since his arms had grown strong enough to get up the mainsail and lend a decent haul to a net. Matt had had no choice in the matter, but it had never occurred to him to want anything different. His father was a hard master, but Matt knew that his lot was far better than that of most of the smacks' boys, who did nothing but mend and clean, make tea, and get beaten for their pains. From the start Matt had been given responsibilities that had forced him to learn fast. If he made mistakes, he knew better than to expect indulgence—he, too, was more than familiar with the business end of his skipper's belt—but at least he had the comfort of knowing that he was learning something. After three years he knew the meaning of the feel of the wind and the message of a chop on the water. He knew what the tide was doing at all hours of the day and night and, more important than any of these, he had learned, and was still learning, the ever-shifting pattern of the offshore shoals which were their fishing grounds. (Having once grounded the smack on an ebb tide, he had had a full four hours until she refloated in which to appreciate both the folly of his mistake and the power of his father's temper.)

Matt was fifteen now, a slender but wiry boy with rough dark hair and the vivid blue eyes of the proverbial sailorman. He had wide-apart cheekbones and a strong chin like his father, brown skin with a sprinkling of freckles, and hands as hard and strong as a man twice his age. With a family of five children to feed, Tom Pullen did not often allow his smack to idle on her mooring. Matt knew what it was to go out on a dawn tide, slipping out to sea while a pale moon still lingered in the sky, and stream the nets before the folk on shore had as much as put their feet out of bed. Sometimes it seemed to him that the whole world consisted only of a few square feet of sprat-slippery deck, an acre of dull-gray shifting sea and the weight of the stow net hanging from the jib halyards.

The wind was on their quarter now and the tide under them. A mile or two away on their port bow they could see where the river estuary divided the shores. Up there among the creeks and saltings and half-submerged islands of the north shore lay the Marshfield moorings, and over the sea wall and up the track was Marshfield village with its rows of fishermen's cottages and the old church ringed round with salty elm. Matt's eyes were on the winking lights.

"Go and ask Aaron to get my baccy off the shelf," his father ordered, pulling out a dirty old pipe.

Tom Pullen always lit up when he was feeling pleased with himself. Matt went forward and put his head in the hatch.

"Baccy for my dad, Aaron."

Aaron was the third hand on *Fathom*, an old man in his sixties who had worked for Tom Pullen before Matt was born. He was a strange character, simpleminded but quite harmless. Not that anyone seeing him about his business would guess at his feeblemindedness, for he knew as much about the job as any skipper in Marshfield. He flung up the pouch of tobacco and Matt took it back aft to his father. He noticed that *Charity* was creeping up on them, but he didn't mention it to his father. Instead he said, "How do you reckon Beckett made the money to buy *Charity*?"

It was a question that was of perennial interest among the Marshfield smacksmen, but Matt had never heard a real answer yet. He knew the trouble his father always had to raise enough money for new rigging or a new sail, and it didn't seem possible that a man could find the fortune necessary for a new boat. Not by the Pullen family standards at least.

"Old Beckett does a might more than fish with his boat, especially in the wintertime," Tom Pullen said mysteriously.

"What do you mean?" Matt asked, looking up curiously.

"I doubt if there's a wreck off this coast that hasn't had Beckett sailing in for the pickings," Tom Pullen said.

"Salvage, you mean?"

"There's some call it salvage. Piracy I call it, as far as Beckett's concerned. It's not lives he's after saving. More like a few bolts of silk or some such."

So that was the explanation, Matt thought. He looked back at *Charity* again, not so admiringly this time, and at the shadow of her skipper at the helm, the taciturn, black-haired, black-eyed Beckett. Beckett was no native of Marshfield. He had come there with his wife and brothers about five years ago and had made few friends since, and most people in

Marshfield said he'd chosen the place to live in because it was conveniently remote from the meddlesome habits of the Marchester customs men.

The smacksmen regarded him with suspicion and a certain amount of grudging respect, for he was clever. Too clever, Tom Pullen had often said, to be a smacksman. No one knew where he had come from, but there were plenty of rumors to the effect that the Sussex excise men had got to know him too well; that Essex was his bolthole. His very reticence bore out these rumors. No one fished more ardently than Beckett when the revenue cutters were in the neighborhood, but when they were not, *Charity* sometimes set her sails on unexplained journeys and disappeared for a week or two at a time. If this was smuggling, as rumor had it, Matt knew no more than anyone else, but salvaging was another matter.

Matt knew plenty about salvaging. He knew that for as many boats that went out to save life, as many would be hanging around a wreck to see what they could gain from the other's misfortune. And in the wintertime on this treacherous east coast, with its shifting sand bars stretching way out to sea, there were plenty of disasters. Word got about quickly. He had often heard mention of a wreck among the men as they rowed out to start the day's work (or night's work, according to the tides). "There's a brig on the Gunfleet," or "East Indiaman went on the Burrows last night." He had seen signal guns and distress rockets pierce a gale with a spluttering flash of despair. He had seen collier brigs aground only a mile or so off Marshfield, and he had seen survivors brought ashore and bodies washed up on the saltings.

Twenty years ago Aaron had been one of these casualties. Two days and nights clinging to the rigging of a water-

logged brig in seas too steep to let the rescue boats approach
had unhinged his mind, and Tom Pullen had taken pity on
him when he had eventually been brought ashore, gibbering
and incoherent, and had taken him into his own house.
When the growing family had started to strain the small
Pullen cottage at the seams, Aaron had moved in to lodge
at a neighbor's two doors away. Matt could never remember
a time when Aaron had not been waiting silently on the sea
wall for his father when the smacks were ready to put out.

Matt stifled another yawn. It was getting dark and behind
them across the restless gray hummocks of the sea the
smacks' lights traced a pattern in the dusk. Where the sun
had disappeared, landward, the sky was hard and yellowish
with wind. It would blow up strong later. He was glad he
would be in bed by then, and listening to the roar of it from
the warmth of his blankets.

He was happy enough to stand, chin down, watching the
glow of his father's pipe while *Fathom* moved steadily inshore towards the mouth of Marshfield creek. The tide was
flooding: the creek was a wide inhospitable expanse of water
under the first of the stars. Tall withies sticking up forlornly
off the banks marked the oyster layings. Apart from those,
there was nothing: a flat horizon where the saltings, or
marsh, took over from the water, a colorless dusk, a landscape of sad nothingness with a smell of mud to it and a taste
of salt to the lips. At low tide the serpentine channel was
the only way in. The sea ran out to leave banks of gleaming
mud on either hand, the withies naked here and there and
the sandpipers and herons wading on the water line.

The smacks went up on the flood, *Fathom* and *Charity*
side by side, behind them the *Miranda* of George Firmin's,
a young skipper who had taken over his father's smack when
the old man had been washed overboard and drowned in

a big sea. In spite of his comparative youth—he was only twenty—George Firmin landed a bigger catch than most over the year. He was a good friend of Matt's. Matt watched him now, by using the strongest path of the tide, gain a boat's length on *Fathom*. Even if *Miranda* was no prizewinner among the Marshfield smacks, there was very little on the wind or in the water that George didn't put to good use. But even *Miranda* could not tell on the confident *Charity*.

"Ah, the old devil," Tom Pullen swore as the new smack swung across his bows into the winding arm of the home creek. *Fathom*'s bows barely cleared Beckett's rudder.

"Serve him right if you'd taken a gout out of those new planks of his," George Firmin remarked as *Miranda* crept alongside.

"Aye, he'll thrust once too often," Tom Pullen snorted.

The creek narrowed. In the dusk Matt could see the "hard" where the track from the village came down to the water. First boat home moored nearest to it and her catch was soon away, loaded into the dinghy, rowed to the hard, and transferred to the carts that were waiting there. Beckett's anchor splashed home as Matt ran forward to douse the headsails. Tom Pullen turned up into the wind and Matt let go *Fathom*'s anchor. Aaron was already rolling out the sprat barrels and Tom was pulling the skiff up against the stern. It was Matt's job to stow sails while the two men took the catch ashore; then his father would row back for him and they would walk home together. But tonight George gave the *Fathom* a shout.

"No need to come back for your boy, Tom! I'll bring him ashore when I'm cleared up."

"Very good, George."

The laden skiff pulled away and Matt tidied up the deck. By the time he had finished, George was sculling across to him from *Miranda* with the last of his catch. George's two younger brothers who crewed for him, Clem and Albert, were already ashore.

"Ready?"

"Coming." Matt slipped down into the dinghy and settled himself on the center thwart. As George sculled for the hard Matt watched the last comers of the fleet reaching up the creek in the distance, dark shadows in the mist that was creeping across the marsh. He wondered vaguely what George wanted him for. There was more in this lift, surely, than mere comradeship. At the end of twelve hours' fishing one did not make such gestures for no reason.

The hard was a tangle of skiffs and barrels, and the air reeked of fish and sweating horses.

Matt waited for George on the sea wall while he disposed of his catch. George caught him up and the two of them walked in silence until they came to the gate of the Pullen cottage. Then George said, "Do you reckon your dad would let you off a day's work tomorrow? I'm taking the old smack up to Marchester to collect her new mainsail. I thought you might fancy the trip. Clem said he'd work for your dad."

Matt stopped with his hand on the gate.

"D'you think he would?" he breathed.

"Aye. You tell your dad Clem will wait for him by the

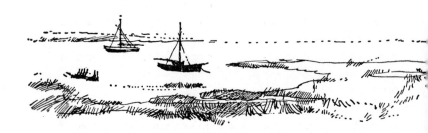

hard in the morning. I'll be leaving on the last of the water so's we get the flood up the big river. You be on *Miranda* about eleven."

"Yes. I'll be there."

Matt's heart felt as light as a bird's as he walked down the path between the cabbage rows to the light shining out of the cottage door. A day off work in any circumstances was reason enough for rejoicing, but a sail up to Marchester into the bargain was enough to start him tingling with anticipation. Marchester was Matt's metropolis. He had never been, nor was he likely to go, to London, although it was only a river away, a day's trip with the wind fair; but a city more exciting than Marchester did not come within the bounds of Matt's imagination. Marchester's riverside was lined at all times with brigs and barquentines, schooners, steam tugs, packets, and revenue cutters. The quaysides were thronged with sailors; her warehouses fragrant with tea, spices, oranges, and wool. There was a smell of tar down there, of rotting bilge water and rats, of sweet new canvas and pale new rope. In the yards that occupied most of the banks the wood was stacked for weathering. There were hulls on the stocks, and strange new shapes of hulls with cutaway stems and strange pinched bows like the curled nostrils of a frightened horse: racing yachts for Lord M. and the Earl of S.—these strange-minded "nobs" from London who sailed for pleasure, a new race of sportsmen looked at askance by the smacksmen. Matt knew of all the boats that were building; he knew that he would see the newly launched *Good Fortune* at her mooring and that the *Euphrosyne* would be home from the East Indies. And a day with George was something to look forward to, too. Matt rarely had the opportunity for developing friendships.

He pushed open the kitchen door and blinked into the

lamplight. His father was already sitting at the table, attacking an enormous bowl of onion soup, and his mother was dishing up at the fire. Matt looked warily at his father, trying to discern his mood, for he knew by experience that his father's moods could change rapidly. Tom Pullen had a fierce temper, but it usually burned itself out as quickly as it kindled. He grumbled a lot, but he was also generous,

quick to forget a wrong, and fond of a good laugh. On board Matt knew where he stood with his father; at home, when it came to asking favors, he wasn't so sure. He moved nervously across the stone flags and stood by the table.

"Please, Father, George asked me to go to Marchester tomorrow. He's taking *Miranda* to collect a new sail and he says Clem'll go on *Fathom* if you let me go."

Tom Pullen looked up briefly. "Oh, and what's the matter with Clem going to Marchester and you coming along with me as usual, might I ask?" he asked sarcastically, wiping a piece of bread round his plate.

"I—I don't know. I suppose he thought I'd like the trip if Clem didn't go."

"Oh, let the boy go," Matt's mother said suddenly and unexpectedly, putting his dinner on the table before him. "Don't play cat and mouse with him at this time of the day. How often does he have a chance to see a bit of life?"

"And how often do I have the chance, I'd like to know," his father retorted. "The boy's got to learn you don't get no days off when you fish for a livelihood."

"Ah, you had plenty of time off when you were a boy, and if it wasn't given you, you took it, so don't act so high and mighty. Besides, if he goes, he can call on his Uncle Albert. It's time he saw a bit of this family, considering he's my own brother."

"And a pompous old fool he is, too," grumbled Tom Pullen.

"Do you mean I can go?" Matt asked anxiously.

"Yes, of course you can go," his mother said. "And don't you call my brother a pompous old fool in front of the boy, Tom Pullen—even if he is."

Matt glazed blissfully down at his plate. Even the condition of a visit to his Uncle Albert was not enough to dull his victory (it could be made as brief as possible). He could hardly believe his good fortune. His mother, scooping up Tom's empty plate, smiled at Matt over her husband's head.

"It'll give you a lie-abed tomorrow, eh, Matt? George won't be leaving at the crack of dawn."

"Eleven, he said," said Matt.

"Do you good," said his mother.

Matt's mother often thought he worked much too hard for a mere boy. She wished their way of life could give him an easier time, and wondered quite often whether he wouldn't have done better working for his Uncle Albert's business in Marchester. The offer had been made, and Albert had been offended when the boy had turned it down, but Matt had always wanted to fish with his father and his father had wanted it, too. Matt never complained because the only days off he had were when the weather was too bad to go out (or on the rare occasions when there was no breath of wind to stir a sail), and his mother was beginning to reconcile herself to the fact that Matt, like most of the boys in the village and their fathers before them, was dedicated to the sea; that he would live—and likely enough die—on it, and no word of hers would ever change the fact.

"I'll put a clean shirt out for you," she said. "You've got to look respectable if you meet your Uncle Albert."

"I'll be working, Mother," Matt reminded her, uncomfortable at the thought of such finery.

"You'll see him first and work after," his mother said tartly. "He never sees any of this family but they're smelling of sprats and got mud on their breeches."

"That'll be the day when Albert gets mud on his breeches," Tom Pullen said with a grin. He never troubled to hide the fact that he had no great opinion of his wife's brother. Albert considered that his sister had married beneath herself and as he, in his turn, never lost an opportunity to patronize, there was no love lost between the two men.

Matt got on with his dinner, hugging his excitement to him. He felt secure now; the promise had been given. Tonight was no ordinary night. Matt was not so hardened that he could not feel a wild, childish thrill of anticipation at the thought of the morning. He hadn't felt that kind of excitement since the smack race last summer when George Firmin had beaten Beckett by the length of a bowsprit.

He went up to bed dreamily, listening to the buffeting of the wind across the saltings and the familiar creaking of the old gable end which faced the sea.

The Good Fortune

Miranda had a fair wind up the Marchester river. With Matt at the helm she butted along with the water rustling under her bows, one reef tucked into her old red mainsail.

The four-mile run along the coast had been exhilarating. Without a catch to bother about, Matt had enjoyed sailing for sailing's sake. He had kept the smack well offshore, knowing how the shoals ran out to catch the unwary, and an occasional sea had jumped over the bows and sluiced across the deck with a roar, so that George grinned and shouted: "How's the clean shirt?" Matt grimaced. He was going to be a bit damp for Uncle Albert, but who cared? He was picturing himself as young Lord Pullen on his racing yacht, *Miranda,* sailing for a wager. If *Miranda* had been a yacht, he might not have got his feet so wet, but that didn't worry him. At a time like this he could understand why rich men sailed for pure pleasure, a fact that was a mystery to the majority of smacksmen, although they didn't hesitate to take advantage of the jobs the new sport offered. In the summer all the young men who had the opportunity laid up their smacks to work as crew on a racing cutter or a cruising yacht. That was Matt's ambition, in spite of the fact that his father wasn't likely to approve.

As *Miranda* sailed on, the river grew narrower. Matt had to watch what he was doing, for there was a collier brig on their heels and, not far behind that, a laden Thames barge. Nothing was coming down, for the tide was still making; Matt reckoned they would be dropping their anchor at just about high water. The channel was a winding one, but soon the quays and roofs of Marchester appeared beyond the trees and Matt saw mast tops against the sky. George had gone below to get a meal and shouted up, "It's Melville's yard we want, on the starboard bank," and as *Miranda* slipped on, Matt kept his eyes open for the Melville sign. A bend in the river brought the wind on to his bow and he started to beat, his eyes darting about to take everything in. Colliers were unloading on the port bank; ahead of him, moored in midstream, a revenue cutter was just starting to swing on the turning tide. Beyond that he could see the raking masts of a brigantine at anchor and, beyond that again, the fine bows of one of the new racing cutters.

George put his head out of the hatch. "That's Melville's, above the cutter. If you put her in line, she won't dry out."

Matt nodded. He put *Miranda* about as the revenue cutter blocked their passage and the smack scuttled away across the river. Two barges were coming down now. He made two short tacks to give them room and then went neatly across between the brigantine and the racing cutter. The cutter was so lovely and so unlike any ship that he had seen before that he stood at the helm hypnotized as *Miranda*'s mast slid past the great gleaming bowsprit above him. A flashing of gilt work on the clipper bows dazzled him with its artistry, the flawless paintwork of the topsides, white as a seagull's wing, made him blink. Chain plates gleamed; new varnish on the mast was pale gold against the sky. A boy was standing on the deck, leaning on the rail, a boy about his own age, and as Matt held *Miranda* on her course for the far bank the two of them looked at each other, and for a moment their eyes held.

For no reason that he could think of, the exchange embarrassed Matt. A grave, intelligent face, dark, thoughtful eyes: the boy was as handsome as the cutter herself. For the first time in his life Matt was aware of a surge of jealous resentment at the comparison that had been forced. *Miranda*, tarred and workaday, stinking of sprats, was an all too plain indication of his own station in life. He, who would have given ten years of his life to work as crew on a boat like that,

was never likely so much as to set foot on the deck where the boy stood so surely. Matt, never having thought much about the privileges of the rich before, vented his sudden spite on *Miranda*'s helm and spun her round out of the path of a ketch that was moving away from Melville's quay. A dinghy full of sprat barrels was now being sculled laboriously across the water ahead of him and to avoid that he had to graze the cutter's stern and go about again. It took two tacks to see him clear and all the time he was conscious of the cool brown eyes following his antics from the deck of the *Good Fortune*. The ship's name was carved and gilded across her stern, and Matt decided crossly that it suited her well, and all who sailed in her, too.

But once *Miranda*'s anchor had run out opposite the boat-yard and George had shouted to Matt to come down and get started on a steaming duff (George fancied himself as a cook), Matt's good nature reasserted itself, and he felt able to enthuse over the lovely racer without rancor.

"She came out of Melville's yard in the spring," George

told him. "They reckon she'll beat anything on the water round here. They're waiting for her owner to come and give her a trial—a Mr. Shelley; he's a diamond merchant or something—I can't remember rightly. He's a keen one for a wager, though, so they're hoping they'll be seeing some hard racing next summer."

"She might be wanting crew?" Matt said softly.

George grinned. "She won't have any trouble getting it either. I hear Beckett's put a word in already—makes out he's a crony of Shelley's."

"Beckett doesn't miss much," Matt said.

"Not if it smells of money."

Matt grinned and put down his bowl. "Perhaps he reckons he might find a diamond or two lying around the saloon!" Then he grimaced. "I suppose I ought to go and see my uncle, and get it finished with. I wish my mother hadn't thought of it."

"Aye—duty, lad. We'll go ashore together. You'll find me in Melville's yard when you come back."

Fortunately Uncle Albert's business premises were only a short walk down the quay. He kept a large grocer's shop in a small street that gave on to the busiest part of the harbor, and a great deal of his trade was tied up with the provisioning of ships. He specialized too in Dutch cheeses, and the smell of cheese in Matt's nostrils was inextricably connected with Uncle Albert, his pale, cold-eyed face peering down over the polished counter as if the person he was seeing was the most inferior breed of worm. At least, that was the expression that usually greeted Matt. It was compounded of pity and exasperation, and it moved Matt to loathe Uncle Albert from the very depths of his feeling. This occasion was no exception.

"Ah, Matt, my boy, what brings you to Marchester? Not bad news, I hope. Are you alone?"

His uncle's face creased with difficulty into a smile of greeting as his assistant's reverent call brought him out into the shop. Matt twisted his knitted boatman's cap uneasily in his hands.

"Yes, Uncle Albert. I just came in with George Firmin. My father let me have the day off work, and my mother said I should call and tell you we're all well at home."

"Ah." Uncle Albert looked faintly disappointed. "You're still fishing, are you, Matt? Earning your keep, I hope?"

"Yes, Uncle." Matt stared at the floor.

"Look up, boy," his uncle commanded. "And stop twisting your fingers. You must take my regards to your dear mother, and tell her I hope she is not too weary with looking after all you children. If ever I can do anything to help her at any time, she has only to ask me."

"We don't need any help," Matt said bluntly.

Uncle Albert frowned angrily, but as he opened his mouth to reply, the shop bell tinkled and a man came in. He was dressed in a nautical fashion, but did not look like a sailor. Uncle Albert immediately crossed over to serve him. The man treated him in a very offhand manner, but Uncle Albert took his order with much smiling and bowing and, when he had finished, escorted him to the door with a last deep obeisance. Then he came back to Matt, looking pleased with himself.

"That was Mr. Shelley's steward, off the *Good Fortune*," he said happily. "He is provisioning for their maiden voyage. A very good customer of mine, Mr. Shelley, a very appreciative man. You have probably heard of him, Matt—Mr. Peregrine Shelley. He is an expert on precious stones, and has worked for the Queen. It is a most distinguished family, and very wealthy. Very wealthy, indeed. You understand I have a very high-class business here, Matt. You were unwise to turn down your chance of working here for me. Your dear mother was very disappointed."

Matt was looking at the floor again so that his uncle would not see from his face how much he despised him.

"I'm afraid I must go now, Uncle. We have the tide to catch and I promised I would only be away a few minutes."

"Very well, my boy. Remember what I said."

Matt was left to see himself to the door, and as soon as he was out in the street again he took a deep breath of relief. To work for his uncle . . . ! The very thought of it made Matt feel faint with horror. If anything should ever happen to his father so that his mother had to ask Uncle Albert for help— that was an unbearable thought. Over my dead body, Matt vowed, as he headed down to the quay. The sight of bare yards and topmasts against the sky put the unsavory meeting out of his head, and in a few moments he was down beside the hulls of the Newcastle colliers, watching the whippers unloading. This wasn't a job he would have fancied doing himself, any more than cutting cheese for Uncle Albert.

He stood watching for a few minutes as the gang of men kept up their constant round of jumping off a wooden platform and climbing back on again. The men held the pulley rope in their hands and with each jump brought a basket of coal jerking up out of the hold. Below on the quay, carts were waiting to take it away, the coal that was carried in a never-ending stream down the East Coast from Newcastle. Matt had had a cousin working on a collier, but he had been lost in a storm several winters back when a hundred and fifty vessels had been wrecked in one night. There was a lot to be said for working inshore, Matt thought, as he made his way back to Melville's.

George had got his new sail and was stowing it into the dinghy when Matt got down to the water. "The wind's too strong to bend it on now. A pity, but she's got to be stretched with a gentler breeze than this," he said.

The sunlight was peering restlessly between flying clouds, and the dinghy smacked across the waves as George rowed her back to *Miranda*. They went aboard and set about stow-

ing the stiff new canvas below. Matt could not help glancing across to feast his eyes on the *Good Fortune*, wondering if he might ever work a passage aboard her. There was no sign of the brown-eyed boy; in fact, the only sign of life was a man putting the finishing touches to the gilding on the bows, sitting in a cradle hung over the side. Matt was just straightening up on the foredeck when he was startled by a yell from across the water. One of the cradle ropes had snapped, and he turned just in time to see the painter go into the water with a loud splash.

Matt's first reaction was to laugh. Then he stood to watch what happened.

The painter went under, and when he came to the surface all he did was shout and thresh about. Then he went under again. Matt stopped grinning and sprinted down *Miranda*'s deck. A deft yank on the rope released the dinghy; he tumbled in and grabbed the oars. The tide plucked the dinghy away from *Miranda*'s stern and in a second he was under the bows of the *Good Fortune*. A glance over his shoulder and he saw an arm break the surface about twenty yards downstream, and at the same moment he saw a slight body dive nimbly off the cutter's stern and start to swim rapidly after the drowning man. Feeling somewhat relieved, Matt rowed after him. Pulling a man in over the stern of the dinghy was something he thought he could manage, but rescuing someone who had already sunk below the surface would, he knew, be beyond him. There was no longer any sign of the painter, and the swimmer submerged as Matt watched, presumably to look for him. His heart pounding anxiously, Matt brought the dinghy round into the tide and waited for him to reappear. What had seemed so amusing only a moment before, now looked like tragedy.

He waited so long that he began to think they were both drowned. Then suddenly a head broke the surface just beyond him. He dug the oars in and sent the dinghy skimming towards it.

"I've—I've got him!"

The rescuer was the boy who had watched Matt bring *Miranda* up the river. If Matt had envied him then, he envied him no longer as the boy struggled to keep his grip on the drowning man in the fast-flowing tide. The man was threshing about in a panic and Matt, dropping his oars, just managed to jump into the stern and grab him by his collar before he went under again. With a desperate heave he dragged him far enough out of the water to get his elbows over the transom. Once supported in that manner, the man stopped struggling and clung on like a limpet, and the boy, with a gasp of relief, swam clear.

"Can you get him aboard?" he called to Matt.

"I can if he'll help himself," Matt replied, and after a few seconds the man recovered his senses enough to heave himself over the stern and collapse in a heap into the bottom of the boat. The boy swam up with a few strong strokes and climbed in after him, settling himself on the stern seat as Matt reached for the oars again.

"We'd better land him at the yard," the boy said coolly. "We'll never get him into the yacht. There's no one else on board to help."

Matt nodded. The tide had carried them well down the river during their struggles and it was a hard pull back. He didn't say anything for the simple reason that he couldn't think of any suitable remark to address to the self-possessed figure before him. He applied himself to his rowing, and the boy pushed back his dripping hair and helped the moaning painter into a sitting position on the duckboards. By the time the man had come to his senses the dinghy was grounding on Melville's hard, and several men who had witnessed the incident came running down to help. Matt stayed where he was while the painter's workmates bore him ashore amid a good deal of excitement. The office clerk was fluttering over Matt's companion, who was still sitting in the stern and looked rather bored with the man's congratulations.

"If it hadn't been for this boy here with the dinghy," he said rather abruptly, "we should both have drowned, so you should spend some of your congratulations on him." He turned to Matt and said rather more politely, "Would you mind rowing me back to the yacht?"

"Of course I will."

"If I may venture to suggest you come ashore and use the premises to dry yourself, sir—" the clerk stammered.

"I have clean clothes on board, thank you."

Matt, realizing the boy was getting impatient with the clerk, pushed off with his oar and headed out towards the *Good Fortune*. He made no effort to start a conversation, but now his companion was looking rather more friendly. Hugging his arms against the cold breeze that was whistling across the river, he leaned forward and said, "Do you live here?"

"No. I live at Marshfield. We're going back now."

"You'll have a rough trip. Do you work on the smack?" He nodded across the water towards *Miranda*.

"I work on my father's smack." Matt explained what had brought him to Marchester on *Miranda*.

"I envied the way you handled that boat this morning," the boy said as they came up under the cutter's stern.

The compliment was so unexpected Matt nearly dropped his oars. He looked up awkwardly, remembering the ungracious thoughts that had been passing through his head at the time, and flushed. The boy smiled as he reached up for the deck.

"If you'd like to come aboard and have a look round—" he suggested.

Matt hesitated. His first thought was to accept—in fact, he could not imagine a thing in the world that he would rather do at that moment—but his sailor's instinct reminded him that there was a tide he must be catching. A glance over his shoulder confirmed his suspicion that George was all ready to go and was only waiting for him to gain the deck before he pulled up the anchor. He shook his head, not bothering to conceal his disappointment.

"We've the tide to catch," he said.

The boy looked disappointed, too, but he was sailor enough to appreciate the situation. He paused, and then he held out his hand.

"I hope we'll meet again. Tell me your name."

"Matt Pullen." Matt grasped the hand and shook it. The boy's fingers were as strong as his own in spite of the fact they were so clean and smooth. Matt smiled and picked up the oars again.

"I hope so, too."

Thoughtfully he rowed back to the waiting smack. The boy had disappeared, the incident was over, but Matt felt that it was an afternoon that would stay in his mind—although for what reason he wasn't sure.

Francis Shelley dropped his wet clothes on the floor for the steward to dispose of and picked out a clean shirt and a pair of trousers from the wardrobe in his cabin. Then, having dried himself and dressed again, he strolled aft into the main saloon and through a porthole he watched *Miranda* sail away down the river. He sighed and flung himself down on the horsehair sofa-*cum*-bunk, where he lay and surveyed the mahogany ceiling, his hands clasped behind his head.

He had been perfectly genuine when he had complimented Matt on his handling of the smack, and he mused now on Matt's astonishment. The boy obviously came from a place where everyone could handle smacks as naturally as they could walk; it had never occurred to him that asses like himself might think it remarkable enough to admire. Francis wondered what it must be like to work on a smack for a living, and wished regretfully that the boy had had more time to spare. He would have liked to have had a talk with him, liked to have learned a bit more about the real sailing.

He's one of them, he thought, and in his mind "them" were all the men whose livelihood was in boats, a fraternity with whom he had come in contact when the *Good Fortune* was put on the stocks for his father. A sensitive boy, it hadn't taken Francis long to sense that "they" thought it was madness to build a boat like the *Good Fortune* for sheer pleasure, that "they" despised his father and his companions when it came to matters of sailing, in spite of the fact that they were in all other matters only too ready to fawn and flatter, like that odious yard clerk and the grocer by the quayside. This, Francis found, was rather disturbing, for sailing was the only thing he had come across in all his life so far that seemed to him really worth doing. He didn't like being treated as an eccentric; he wanted to learn. Matt was the first person he had met on the water who had treated him as an equal, and Francis had liked his direct blue eyes and un-affected silences. Matt was the sort of person he could learn from, he thought, remembering how he had threaded that smack through the crowded water without even looking as if he was thinking what he was doing, and how nimbly he had handled the dinghy to come to his aid.

"Damn that tide," he said aloud.

"I beg your pardon, sir?"

Francis turned and saw the steward standing in the companionway.

"I didn't know you were back," he said. "Can I have some tea?"

"Certainly, sir."

"Did my father tell you what time he was coming down tonight?"

"Mr. Shelley said he would be on the quayside at eight o'clock, sir."

"Very well."

Tomorrow the *Good Fortune* was going on her first trial. Francis smiled at the thought of the lovely cutter feeling the wind in her sails for the first time. She, too, was a newcomer to the water. Perhaps, after all, it would not be too long before he was fit to stand at her helm and sail her out to sea. Together he and the ship would learn what "they" already knew.

The Wreck of the *Seaflower*

A hard winter gave Matt more time at home than he was accustomed to during the next few months. His father grumbled constantly as wild northeasterlies kept him from his spratting. Idleness was not in his nature and he soon had the small kitchen filled with sails for mending and Matt at work with a needle and palm, stabbing reluctantly at the never-ending task. Matt found he had time to think, and he thought about the *Good Fortune* as he sewed, seeing her virgin canvas, white as apple blossom, bearing her downriver in the spring. If his vision of the yacht was fanciful, so indeed did she seem to him now, the dream yacht of a diamond merchant. He could barely believe that he had once had the chance to step aboard. The memory had been drowned in the all too vivid reality of winter spratting. From autumn to Christmas, the spratting season, *Fathom* had pounded her way out day after day to Tom Pullen's favorite haunts and threshed home laden to the decks, awash from stem to stern. But after Christmas, gales had kept the fleet at home and even Tom, saving desperately for a new smack to replace the failing *Fathom*, had been forced to leave his anchor firmly in the mud.

Matt, with only his sewing to occupy him, went to bed

strangely untired. One night he was still awake past midnight, lying with his hands clasped behind his head and
thinking of the boats that were out in this wild weather. In
the other bed the twins, Jack and Joseph, were two inert
humps under the blankets. The twins were still at school and
his sister Anne worked up at the vicarage as a housemaid—
they none of them, with Matt's instincts, listened to the wind
when they were in bed at night. Matt always thought of the
clippers coming up the Channel, the skillingers tossing about
off the Dutch coast, nearly two hundred miles from home,
or the barges caught offshore with a shoal on their lee . . .
somewhere there would be a ship in trouble, and Matt's
nerves grew taut as he pictured a torn sail lashing the darkness, a hull on her beam-ends with the water pouring green
across her hatches. Matt had more imagination than most of
the boys who worked the smacks, and it didn't do him any
good on a night like this. He turned over angrily, and at
that very moment a muffled report came faintly on the wind.

He stiffened, the breath catching in his throat. The next
instant he was out of bed and at the window. The window
faced seawards—in fact, it was separated from the sea only
by an acre of pasture, the sea wall, and a stretch of salting—
and Matt was just in time to see a flash like a ball of fire go
up from the darkness, hover and fade. Pinpointing its position, he made a rapid calculation in his head. Whatever it
was, the ship in distress was not likely to be aground, for the
tide was just about full. More likely it was dismasted, or
merely overwhelmed by the steep seas. In spite of the wind,
the night was not very dark. The moon was nearly full, although it was obscured by cloud, and there was a brightness
over the water which made him think it might not be too
difficult to trace the wreck even if she sent up no more
signals.

While all this was going through his head, the thud of footsteps shook the small cottage from the adjoining room, and the next moment Tom Pullen was in the doorway.

"Matt!"

His father was pulling on his heavy jersey, and behind him his mother was lighting the candles, her face anxious in the warm light.

"You're not taking the boy!" she said, but Matt was already scrambling into his stiff working trousers.

"Aye, I'll need him," Pullen said briefly.

"Why must you go? You—"

"The ship's on our own doorstep, Mary. Besides, there might be something in it for us. The Lord knows we could do with it! If I'd a new smack now, I might leave it to the others."

Matt knew what was in his father's mind: he had obviously decided that to earn some extra money he was going out salvaging. He had been to several wrecks before, but only to help get the crew off. He had never been keen on the salvaging business, aware that his life was more valuable to his family than a bit of extra money. But with *Fathom* failing he had no choice. Matt dragged on his jersey and followed his father downstairs, leaving his brothers chattering excitedly in the bedroom. He felt both scared and excited as he pulled on his heavy leather boots before the fire. His mother, tight-lipped, fetched the smocks from their hooks and handed them over, and in a minute they were at the door and the wind was blasting through the kitchen, snuffing the candles and flaring the embers in the hearth.

"Go back to bed, woman." Tom flung the words over his shoulder to his wife. "We'll be back by dawn."

Tom Pullen had no time for sentiment and this, to him, was a job like any other. But Matt, stumbling through the mud and ruts down the track, had a cold feeling in the pit of his stomach. He was not scared of sailing out to the wreck, but he was scared of what they might see when they got there. All his life he had been familiar with tales of wreck and disaster, but never had he been forced to look upon it at close quarters. He had pulled bodies out of the water before, but he had never seen a man at the point of death, clinging to the rigging of a sinking ship.

They had to brace themselves against the wind as they went over the wall. The tide was still high and their dinghy was afloat. Old Tom took the oars and in a matter of minutes they were alongside *Fathom*'s stern. As Matt made the dinghy fast he heard the splashing of footsteps on the hard behind them, and he turned in time to see a familiar figure silhouetted against the sea wall. They were not the only ones who had heard the rockets go up.

"Look, Father. It's Beckett. Do you think he's going out too?"

"He's not out here to pick mushrooms, boy," his father replied tartly. "Go and get that anchor up. We've no time to lose if he's thinking of poking his nose in."

Matt ran forward to the bows. By the time he had broken it out his father had the staysail up and the smack was away, the water hissing wildly past her bows.

"Reef the mains'l right down. We'll use it once we're out," Tom ordered.

Matt crouched on the deck to sort out the great, stiff, patched bundle of woven flax that was *Fathom*'s motive power, and as he worked, the staysail cracked and swayed up forward, a dark blot against the luminous sky. Stars scudded past the mast, then the clouds came up to swallow them, and the wind tore the water into a seething mass of white.

"What a night! There'll be snow with this before morning." Tom Pullen glanced behind him and thought he heard on the wind the rasping of an anchor chain. "The old devil!" he swore. "He'll be rubbing his hands up there on the helm. Are you ready, Matt? She'll stand it if she doesn't fall to pieces first. We've got to get out there before that devil!"

Matt went up to the main halyards, and in a moment *Fathom* was sailing out of the creek under her reefed main and staysail, and into the fierce sea. The smack could take it all right, but it was hardly a pleasure to stand up there on her flat bare deck as she buried her bowsprit in and threw the sea in sheets over her back like a played whale. Matt bit his lip, staring out to sea for a glimpse of a light or another rocket, and wondering whether, after all, their journey was to be in vain. No foundering ship would last long in this, nor would a man.

"Can you see Beckett, eh?" his father asked. "Keep your eyes skinned, boy."

Hanging on to the shrouds, Matt obediently scanned the darkness in all directions. Astern, he could see a black object on the water that could only be *Charity*'s mainsail; ahead he could see nothing but lumping seas.

"He's following us," he reported briefly.

His father swore.

"If that ship has gone down, we won't be the only ones wasting our time out here."

"Look!" Matt cried suddenly. "There's a light out there! That will be her. I can see it now—a white one—wait a bit. There it is! Do you see it?"

"Aye. That's it." Tom's eyes were on the compass now. Matt felt himself shivering, but he wasn't sure if it was from cold or apprehension. The light was a good way to port of them, and as *Fathom* came round, burying her lee rail, Matt saw *Charity* creeping up astern. She must have seen the light, too, for she had also changed course, and Matt guessed she would reach the ship at just about the same time as *Fathom*. His father was muttering under his breath, but he was powerless to hold *Charity* at bay.

"The old shark," he muttered. "If there's any survivors around, they won't get much comfort from Beckett, I'll wager. I'll laugh if it's only an old ketch full of potatoes and all the gear rotten into the bargain. Like as not, it is. No one with any sense would be sailing tonight."

When a ship was foundering, not only was her cargo fair game for a "salvager," but her gear was likely to be stripped as well. In theory, salvage was delivered to the official receiver of wrecks in Marchester, but in practice, as Matt well knew, it very rarely saw the insides of the Customs House. Tonight his father, like Beckett, would be looking for something that would make him a bit of money, and whoever got there first would take the pickings.

"I can see her," Matt said suddenly.

Above the waves ahead he had a glimpse of a torn sail at a listing mast. It was only a glimpse, but it was right on their bows. *Fathom* plunged on and Matt, shaking the water from his face, strained his eyes forward. The darkness was a maze of shifting indistinguishable shapes: what was a torn sail one moment was a breaking crest the next. Matt, his throat tight and dry with apprehension, stared until he could see masts everywhere.

"It must have lost its light within the last few minutes, else we'd be seeing it by now," his father growled.

"Look!" Matt said. His face was white under his streaming souwester. "Oh, God, look at that!"

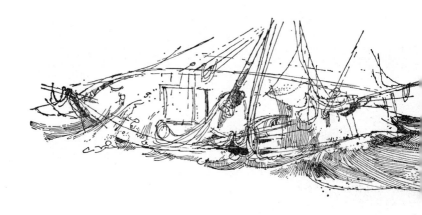

"Aye, that's the ship." Satisfaction mingled with the pity in Tom's voice, but Matt, who had never seen a foundering ship at close quarters before, thought his heart would turn over as *Fathom* rode up on a big sea and faced the wrecked ship squarely over a few hundred yards of pounding water. It was the sight he had conjured up in his mind a hundred times when the wind was fighting to take the roof off from over his head back home, the sight of a ship on her beam-ends, her ballast shifted, her bows fighting in vain to ride the seas that were overwhelming her. Tom hadn't been far wrong when he had prophesied a "ketch full of potatoes." The ship was a small one, a West Countryman by the look of her, and it was obvious to them both that she was very close to going down. She was listing at an angle of about forty-five degrees, and the sea was sweeping her decks so that her hull was all but invisible; the great proud mast looked to Matt like a stag holding a pack of hounds at bay, resisting the seas that leaped to drag her down, dipping and reeling against the black sky. The mizzenmast was gone, and rigging trailed in the sea about her like the hair of a drowning woman.

"We're too late," Matt whispered, when he could find a voice.

"Aye. She's going," his father growled angrily. "There's no one aboard her either that I can see. They must all have been washed overboard by now."

But he didn't put *Fathom* about. She pitched on towards the wreck until the swaying mast was almost above them and the scoured deck rose like a wall across their bows.

"Even Beckett won't be going aboard this one," Tom Pullen said as he turned *Fathom* up into the wind.

Matt touched his arm suddenly.

"Father, there's a man!" he said. "At the foot of the mast."

When he looked again he thought he was mistaken. Tom Pullen tacked *Fathom* back again, and his eyes raked the swilling deck.

"I'm sure it was," Matt said.

The ketch rolled and the mast pulled itself up yet again, and in that instant both of them saw the man on deck. He was lashed to the mast and looked more dead than alive. But as *Fathom* plunged past, they both saw an arm go up and heard a feeble shout above the pounding of the seas. At the

same moment *Charity* loomed alongside out of the darkness
and Beckett shouted to them from the tiller. "She's too far
gone! We've wasted our time."

"Aye, but there's a man aboard her yet," Tom shouted
back.

As *Charity* beat her way to windward, heading for home,
Beckett shouted back over his shoulder: "He'll stay there,
too, as far as I'm concerned!"

Matt's face was ashen. "Father, we can't leave him! He's
alive. He saw us."

Tom Pullen put *Fathom* about again. "Perhaps if we ride
close, he can jump for it."

His eyes anxious, he ran *Fathom* as close as he dared to
the streaming rails. For a moment Matt thought their own
mast was going to touch the great heeling stick above them,
but as his heart missed a beat they were by, and *Fathom* was
reaching out into the open again. The man hadn't moved.

"He's too weak to unfasten himself," Pullen growled.

Matt knew that has father couldn't make up his mind what
to do, and his indecision suggested to Matt that he thought
there was a chance of getting the man off.

"I could take the rowing boat," he pleaded. "There's still
time. She hasn't gone over any farther."

"Aye, and kill yourself," Tom muttered.

He looked at Matt as he stood at his shoulder, braced
against the helm. It was a searching look, as if he hadn't seen
him before.

"I don't like to leave the man," he said.

"I'll go," Matt said. "I'll get him."

At that moment he would rather have drowned himself
than sail away and leave that lone spark of life on the wreck.
To sail away would be to die a thousand deaths. He would
never forget the fervent emotion that moved him as he

turned and grasped the painter. His father said nothing. He could not bring himself to encourage his son, yet neither could he abandon the man on the wreck.

Matt pulled the heavy skiff up.

"Take your boots off," his father ordered. "Your jacket, too—you can't get any wetter. If you go in, I'll throw you a line."

He spoke curtly out of his fear. Matt obeyed, and then got down into the pitching skiff. His father cast off the warp, throwing it down onto his bows, and suddenly Matt found himself alone in the nightmare sea with all his zeal draining away through the soles of his bare feet. The skiff felt like a nutshell. He dug in the oars and braced himself as a sea broke over him, and the water swilled into the skiff over his ankles. For the first time in his life he knew pure physical fear; as *Fathom* reached away into the darkness he felt sure that he would never come through this ordeal alive. The skiff rode up on the pitching seas. Clenching his teeth, Matt dug in the oars and got the bows round into the seas, then he started to force his way towards the stern of the sinking ketch. The oars clawed desperately at the water, and Matt's heart lifted again as he saw that he was making progress. If he had felt abandoned when *Fathom* left him, he wondered what the poor wretch aboard the ketch was feeling, having seen (as he must) his companions drowned. Matt braced himself on the oars until at last he was alongside the heeling rudder, and as he hung on, looking up at the dreadful angle of the half-submerged transom, he realized that his hardest task was only just beginning—to fight his way forward along that sloping deck to the mast.

He made the painter fast to a deck rail, feeling as if his arms were being torn out of their sockets in the process, and then scrambled up out of the bucketing boat onto the top of the rudder. As he came up over the transom, the appalling shambles of the doomed ship was brought home to him. Debris was everywhere: the remains of the splintered mizzen, broken hatch covers, a crushed ship's boat, all lay in a tangle of shredded sail and rigging across the decks, and with each new sea that broke over the side something shifted

or rolled or groaned in that shining mass of desolation, so that Matt could not see where to put a foot. He hung on to the sternpost until an ominous roll reminded him that time was short, and then, trusting in providence and the weather rail, he started to clamber his way forward, hanging on like a monkey.

He was only about halfway when a big sea broke over the rail in his face, knocking him flat on his back. His scrabbling hands clutched at the air. Helpless, he rolled over and over down the sloping deck and into the water where, when he was completely submerged, the lee rail caught him. Choked with sea water, he clung for his life to the capping rail until he gradually managed to pull himself upright out of the water again. There he stood gasping for what seemed minutes, convinced that at any moment the deck above him, which reared up like a wall, was going to fall and roll him under forever. But as he got his breath his courage came back and he started to clamber forward again, inching up over the splintered boom and pulling himself forward by the trailing ribbons of sailcloth. Now he could see the mainmast, and he let out a gasping shout. He didn't stop to wonder what he should do if the man was unconscious. The fact that he had completed his journey to the mast was satisfaction enough for the moment.

But the man wasn't unconscious. He was staring at Matt with red-rimmed eyes, his lips trembling, his hands shaking as they plucked at the ropes that held him.

"Thank God!" he said. "Thank God you've come."

Matt scarcely looked at the man's face. He had pulled out his knife and was hacking through the ropes that tied him to the mast. The man's hands were cut and bleeding and it was no wonder that he couldn't have loosed himself. They were clutching at a small leather bag that was roped to him.

Matt nearly cut the rope by mistake and the man gripped
the bag to him convulsively.

"Come on!" Matt said breathlessly. He tore the ropes away.
Now that the man was freed he felt suddenly more concerned with his own life than the man's. The ship was at
such an angle now he knew she would roll under at any
moment. The fear that he had fought down until now, rose
in his throat like sickness and he turned blindly back up
the streaming deck, scrabbling for fingerholds in the deck
seams. The man followed him, driven by the same panic.
Matt caught the bulwarks with his bloody fingers and clung
on. He could not see the stern for sail tatters and spray; he
only thought it was a mile away as he swung and sweated
along his handhold, one moment splitting his toes on the
torn deck, the next moment swinging and gasping under a
deluge of water with only the solid wood under his palm to
tell him he was still with the ship. He knew the man was
behind him, although how he found the strength in his
exhausted state he never knew. He could hear the man's
moans of pain and exhaustion, and he could feel the deck
under his bare feet quivering as the seas pounded the hull.
The quivering was the ship's mortal pulse. The timbers were
straining and groaning as Matt's hand closed over the sternpost and as he pulled himself over onto the rudder—which
was almost flat and easy as a table—the deck cracked over
his head with a rending of torn wood and a near-human
groaning that turned his heart over. White to the lips, he
slithered down into the dinghy. It was waterlogged, but a
haven of peace after the chaos above it. Frantically he hacked
at the painter with his knife, and as the rope strands parted
he held the boat against the rudder as his companion col-
lapsed into its stern. And even as his hands relaxed their
grip he saw that the rudder was moving, sliding away from

him sideways under the water. The big mast had gone, the remains of the sails hung like gray weeds for a minute on the waves, until at last the split hull surrendered. The water consumed her. It ran into her torn decks and pressed her down. The keel rose, the sea came worrying at it, breaking white in a flurry of triumph along its whole length, and within half a minute the ship had disappeared.

Matt sat in the dinghy holding the gunwales with both hands. He was sobbing with relief and exhaustion, but he didn't know it at the time. The man he had rescued was a moaning heap in the stern, clutching the leather bag; he meant no more to Matt now than a sack of potatoes. It was the ship that was in his mind. He felt as if his heart had gone down with it, for he had no more feeling left in him than a piece of wreckage. He could see nothing in the darkness save the white heads of breaking waves. There was no sign of *Fathom*. Beckett had gone, and the dinghy, heavy with water, slid awkwardly across the seas.

Matt got the oars into the rowlocks, but his hands were so sore he couldn't row. Anyway, he didn't know where to row to.

How long it was before *Fathom* loomed over them he never knew. He heard his father shout, and he heard the slatting of the mainsail as it came up into the wind. The next moment a rope fell into the dinghy almost on his knees and he made it fast, blunderingly, and crawled into the bows.

"Get aboard!" he heard his father shout.

The man in the stern, roused by the voices, was clambering hastily across the thwarts. His instinct of self-preservation was obviously well developed, but he froze as Tom Pullen railed at him from above.

"Take your time, man! Wait till the boy's aboard! You'll turn the thing over if you don't keep down."

Matt felt his father's strong arms hauling him up over the transom and his voice warm and husky in his ears, "Good boy! Good boy!" He grasped the gunwale and stumbled onto the deck, and in a moment the stranger had joined him. The mainsail filled again and the water streamed away under the bows, creaming white but no longer menacing. It was the familiar song of *Fathom* roaring for home. Matt could have kissed her worn old decks.

"Get below, boy, and light the stove. I've no need of you on deck."

His father's voice was gentler than Matt had ever heard it. It gave him, suddenly, an urge to laugh as he swung down into the black pit that was *Fathom*'s fo'c'sle and groped round for the candles. The light flared and he put his hands round the warm flame. They were numb and raw and aching, but he didn't feel them. He was at home with the smell of *Fathom*'s cramped cuddy—a stench of fish and stale smoke and cutch-stained smocks—and the pounding at the bows only meant to him now that they were on their way home and his fear could be forgotten. He fumbled about with the rusty old stove and soon had some of the stacked driftwood blazing in the bars. Smoke belched out as the wind blew down the chimney, but Matt was used to a fair amount of "atmosphere" below, and it didn't worry him as he crouched down before it. His clothes steamed and his joints ached. He was shivering and burning at once and his eyes reddened and stung with the smoke, but he felt perfectly content, drowsy now. He knew that if he lay down on the floor, he would fall asleep immediately.

After a little while the man he had rescued came down the companionway and joined him in front of the fire. Matt had a good look at him for the first time. He was surprised to see that he wasn't dressed like a sailor. His clothes were those of a well-off countryman, slightly shabby but of good materials. His hands, which still held the precious leather case—although not quite so convulsively now—were soft and well kept. He was about fifty, but lean and fit; his features suggested intelligence and a certain authority. But after his adventures aboard the wreck he seemed numbed. He crouched over the fire, but he said nothing. He hardly seemed to see Matt.

Matt gave him the best place at the fire, easing himself back and wedging himself against the bunk, bracing his feet in front of him, for *Fathom* was sailing at a fierce angle and pitching wildly as she went. The wind was still shrieking in her shrouds; loose halyard ends tapped frantically above,

and all the time the waves pounded her hull and broke over her decks with solid thuds. Listening to it all from the cuddy was hardly soothing, but Matt had an unusual sense of detachment. The hatch was shut. He was isolated from the turmoil outside, and it had never happened to him before. He had never sat idle by the stove before when *Fathom* was sailing. He had always been on deck, at hand to obey his father's orders, and this unprecedented privilege emphasized his sense of being set apart tonight. Certainly, he had never experienced an adventure like this before. As he grew warmer Matt began to feel secretly rather pleased with himself.

But his princely exemption from duty was not fated to last long.

"Matt! Come here."

He scrambled to his feet, flung his smock over his head, and hurried up on deck. After the brightness of the fire he could see nothing outside. It was several seconds before he realized that they were just coming into the mouth of the creek.

"We'll have to drop the hook," his father said. "We've got the ebb against us. We'll bide here till the tide turns, then go up on the flood. Get the sails off her."

He turned *Fathom* up into the wind and Matt was fumbling with his skinned fingers at the swollen ropes, muttering with pain and vexation. His father's voice was back to normal. The excitement was over and Matt felt very tired and sore. He let the staysail down, roughly lashing the stiff wet sail, and then the anchor went out, the gaff came down, and *Fathom* stood snubbing her chain angrily in the darkness like a bridled horse.

Tom Pullen dropped down into the hot pit of the cuddy

and Matt followed him, bracing himself against the smack's rolling. Tom Pullen, not a patient man, wasted no time in sounding the stranger.

"You were a passenger on the old ketch then?" he suggested hopefully. Matt knew what was in his mind. By the man's dress he was not a poor man.

The man looked up from the fire.

"Aye, we were sailing to Marchester, my wife and I," he said. "We left Plymouth on Saturday."

"Your wife was with you?" Tom said. "Poor soul, God rest her."

"Aye, God rest her," the man whispered. "God rest them all."

Tom Pullen didn't press the man further, but in a quiet, broken voice, the survivor told them how a sea had swept the woman away before he had thought to tie her to the mast for safety, and how seven of the crew were thrown into the sea when a boat they had lowered capsized only a yard or so off the ketch.

"They tried to make me go with them, but I thought it would be safer to stay with the ship. I—I thought help would come sooner. Two men stayed behind with me, but I don't know what—what became of them. I didn't see anything— until your smack came. I was thinking—of my wife."

"You were going to Marchester on business, sir?" Tom Pullen queried after a pause.

"I was going to Marchester to live," the man said. "I had sold my business in Devon. I have two daughters in Marchester and when we sold up, my wife and I decided to come back to Essex to live. We had all our furniture in the hold of the *Seaflower*, everything I possessed was in that ship. My wife—my money—"

He put his hand on the leather bag that lay in his lap.

"I would have done better to have looked to my wife. This is of little use now."

Tom Pullen licked his lips. He wasn't a soft man—none was blunter when the talk was of money—but he was human enough now to hold his tongue. Matt knew, when he had jumped down into the cuddy and opened up the conversation, that his first query had only been intended as a preamble to business: how much was a man's life worth? But now, in the face of this man's hopeless but dignified grief, he couldn't find the words to ask his question. He looked down at the fire and mumbled awkwardly.

The survivor straightened his shoulders. His eyes were shrewd suddenly.

"What were you fishing for tonight?" he asked.

"It wasn't sprats," said Tom curtly.

"You've got a brave boy there," the man said. "What do you reckon your catch was worth?"

Tom shrugged. "It's the price of a new smack I'm after, else I wouldn't be risking my life in a sea like this. The price to start her building would satisfy me, sir."

"To start her building? You can have the money to finish her, too. I've not much use for it now."

Matt knew that for twenty-five pounds Melville would put a smack on the stocks and take the rest when she was sailing. For a hundred pounds he would build one of *Fathom*'s size, complete with spars and sails; that was the money his father must find, eventually. Matt sat up as the man opened his leather bag. He had heard what the man had said, but the fact that he was actually intending to give his father a hundred pounds was too fantastic to have any meaning.

The bag was full of chinking cloth moneybags. The man

took out two, opened them, and poured a heap of sovereigns onto the bunk. They glowed softly in the candlelight, and Matt stared.

"A hundred, for my life," the man said.

Tom was as spellbound as his son. He said nothing. His mouth hung open. It was the first time Tom Pullen had ever been at a loss for words.

The man shut the leather bag with a snap and said, "Take them. You've earned them."

"A hundred pounds!" Tom said. "It wasn't worth all that!"

"You're belittling me, sir, if you say my life isn't worth a hundred pounds," the man said. "Take it. You need a new smack by the feel of it. You've done a good night's work tonight."

"That I have, sir!" Tom Pullen ran his hands tenderly over the money. His hands were shaking and his lips were dry. He hadn't the voice to say any more.

Matt just stared. A new smack! No wonder his father was speechless! Matt couldn't help thinking of Beckett, and it made him want to laugh out loud. If Beckett had known! Soon they would be sailing in a ship like *Charity* with new sails hard against the sky. Matt saw the ship as he stared at the pile of sovereigns. He saw Melville's yard and the frames of the new smack, the piles of wood shavings and the smell of them mixed with tar and oakum. He said nothing, for the business was between his father and the man off the wreck, but his mind was roving like a terrier. His eyes went from his father's face to the stranger's, and back to the pile of money. He had never seen more than ten sovereigns together before; he saw each one in the gleaming stack as a spar, a plank, a shackle, a bowsprit. . . .

In the hot smoky fo'c'sle he dozed from exhaustion until

his father was stirring him with his boot and shouting, "The tide's flooding, boy. Get up on deck, or your mother will be ordering a black dress."

Dawn was just breaking. The flood pushed sullenly inland between banks of steel-blue mud. It was bitterly cold and a few flakes of snow touched the deck like a pigeon's feathers. *Fathom* worked reluctantly up the narrow channel, tacking from mud flat to mud flat, touching occasionally, stubbornly working her way up between the silent fleet. It was nine o'clock before they got back to the cottage, and Mary Pullen was waiting for them, smiling with relief in the doorway.

Tom Pullen's Jibe

The survivor of the *Seaflower* stayed at the Pullen cottage for two days until his son-in-law from Marchester, having received a message by way of Uncle Albert, came to collect him. Mary Pullen cared for him with quiet compassion, satisfied that her own menfolk had come to no harm. Matt's young body had long ago become hardened to drenching and cold, and his experiences had not hurt him. His mother sensed some strange new excitement in his manner when he came home, and she put it down to his adventure at sea. It wasn't until later that she learned about the money, and it wasn't until the survivor had departed for Marchester that the family felt able to celebrate openly. After all, their good fortune was a direct outcome of their visitor's grief, and while he was under their roof it would have been brutal to rejoice.

But after he had left, the story went round the village like wildfire. Matt was already something of a hero, in spite of the fact that his father's account of the rescue was a terse and understated as a doctor's prescription. Fertile imagination filled in the details and Matt was given a back-slapping reception wherever he went, which embarrassed him so acutely that he didn't venture up to the village again until the gossips found something else to interest them. The fishermen, though, could guess accurately enough at what *Fathom* had accomplished that bitter night, and the general opinion was that the Pullens had earned their new smack. The only man who didn't go out of his way to congratulate them was Beckett.

"He'd have gone aboard quick enough if he'd known there was a hundred pounds to be got out of it," George Firmin said. "He's as brave as they come if he's being paid for it."

George made no secret of the fact that he was delighted at Beckett's discomfiture.

If Beckett knew he was the laughingstock of the village, he made no sign. He went about his work silently and Matt always felt uncomfortable when he was near him. He mistrusted the man and, for some reason, he felt afraid of him. He felt that if the man could gain by doing somebody, including Matt himself, any harm, he wouldn't hesitate to do it. He was a ruthless man, and completely without pity. It did not help to know that Beckett had a good reason for disliking the Pullens: a hundred-pound reason, along with the knowledge that he was being laughed at.

When the gales round the coast had blown themselves out Tom Pullen sailed round to Melville's yard at Marchester to order the new smack. Matt went with him, eager for another glimpse of the big river with all its traffic, and for another look at the *Good Fortune*. The big cutter was out of the water, propped up on legs in the yard, and certainly no dream: Melville scarcely had space for his building. Even Tom Pullen, with business on his hands, stopped to have a look at the fantastic creature with her clipper stem and new-fangled overhang, the enormous lead keel some ten feet from the water line and the great scoop of her long fine counter. She was extraordinarily narrow for her fifty-foot length, but her lines, in spite of their strangeness, were very beautiful.

"Oh, Father, she's lovely!" Matt said as they stood on the hard beneath her bows.

"D'you think they'd take a hundred pounds for her, lad? She'd look well with a load of sprats aboard. Turn 'er over, most likely."

Matt grinned. His father was in a mellow mood, one calloused brown hand clasped firmly over the pouch of his money belt, where what he called his *Seaflower* money, the stranger's sovereigns, lay. He liked to feel the weight of them there, at his waist. He wore the belt day and night, and the thought of the new smack was in his mind all the time. For the last five years he had been scraping and saving—without much to show for it—towards the day when *Fathom*'s old garboards would start to let the water in. Now, with the money in his hand, he felt as if those five years had been taken off his life. He felt as carefree as a boy again. He looked at Matt, gazing up at the *Good Fortune* with his mouth open, and felt a warm rush of affection towards his son. It was Matt's courage that had won them the money. He was a good boy. Tom gave him an affectionate cuff. Matt grinned at him, and Tom realized all at once that the boy was growing up fast. It was a man's job he had done on board the foundering ketch, and now Tom noticed that his son's growing shoulders had split a seam in his jacket, that the clear blue eyes were more direct, less hesitant than six months back. The boyish softness round the mouth and jaw was fast disappearing; the scarred hands looked uncommonly competent hitched into the belt round his narrow waist. Tom nodded sagely to himself, and this unusual flash of paternal pride added to his assurance as he headed for Melville's office.

The business didn't take long. Melville knew what Tom Pullen wanted, and Tom knew what Melville would build him. The only disappointment lay in the fact that Melville had so much work in that he couldn't promise the smack for nearly a year at the earliest. To Matt this sounded like a lifetime, but his father was not surprised. Melville built the best smacks on the coast, and his yard was always busy. Tom Pullen's belt was relieved of a quarter of its burden and in half an hour they were picking their way back to the water's edge between the stacks of timber. Melville came with them, a stocky, oldish man with gentle craftsman's eyes.

"What d'you think of this old girl?" he asked as they came under the shadow of the yacht's lean flanks. "They all reckon she'll take some beating next year."

"She's too tender for my liking," Tom Pullen said, eyeing her narrow middle.

"Aye, she's no smack. We built her to the design of some Scotch fellow Mr. Shelley was enthusin' about. My boy was in charge of the building—I think he was frightened I might 'improve' her if I had charge of 'er—I would have, too. But she sails all right. You'd be surprised. We might have a bit of excitement with 'er next summer."

"Who'll be skippering her?"

"Mr. Shelley hasn't appointed anyone yet. There'll be a fair bit of competition round here until he does."

"Aye, it's a nice job. Easier than dragging a trawl."

"There'll be money in it. He's not mean, this Shelley. She'll carry a fair number of crew, too. It's all good for the trade— we're glad of it these days."

"Aye, with all these steamboats coming in, and the mackerel going out," said Tom. "My father made his living off mackerel in his day. He'd starve if he tried it today, I can tell you. Things are changing all the time and none for the better, that I can see."

"Our new smack will be a change for the better," Matt reminded him as he fixed an oar to scull back to *Fathom*. The old fishermen were always talking about how much better fishing was when they were young, how many more sails lay in the creek, how the holds had never been big enough to take the harvests that had lain there for the gathering. Matt thought that probably their memories were somewhat rosy. Now that their new smack was on Melville's list his father would have to admit that their future was brighter than it had been for years. He did admit it, too, when they were reaching back down the river in the bright January sunshine. He stood at the tiller and sang, and *Fathom* lay over and creamed out past the river buoy as if to show that she was not done yet, and Matt whistled as he trimmed the jib sheet.

"We'll call her *Reward,* the new smack, Matt," Tom shouted suddenly, "after the money." And he started to sing again, and Matt thought of *Reward*—an honest name. He thought of standing up there on smooth new deck timbers with the shining varnish of the new tiller under his palm. It was a good sail home with the wind on their quarter fresh from the southeast, and the sun plunging in and out of high fast-moving clouds, glossing the sea all colors from pewter to violet. By the time they got back it was growing dark and as they climbed the rise to the cottage Matt thought he sniffed a scent of spring in the dusk. The evenings were drawing out and the gales were dying down. There would be more of them to come, but not so many in *Fathom*. *Reward* would ride them, tight as a bottle, and *Fathom* would lie upon the mud and rot quietly away as so many of her sisters had done before her. The Marshfield saltings were strewn with the remains of old smacks. Their ribs lay naked on the mud like the carcasses of so many stranded whales.

This was the hardest time of the year now, the two months before spring. The sprats were poor and most of the smacks went out to work off the Kent coast picking up "five-fingers," or starfish, which were sold to the Essex farmers for fertilizer. Some went trawling for plaice in the Swin. It was a hard time and a dangerous one, for it meant the smacks had to be prepared for any weather as they made their exposed journeys out across the estuary and back. Some nights, pounding their way home through the Swin, the deep-water channel north out of the Thames, with *Fathom* heavy-laden and the water breaking continuously across her decks, Matt found himself crossing his fingers and praying for the old hull to hold together until *Reward* was ready, to carry them safely home. It wasn't an easy feeling to be beating through a steep sea in the darkness in a leaking boat. Matt would take it in turns on the pump with old Aaron while his father steered a compass course and occasionally looked out for the gleam of a lighted buoy—not that there were many for all the dangers of that tide-scoured estuary with its maze of shoals. Old Tom had the pattern of the shoals in his head and the courses at his finger tips like all the smacksmen, and Matt, when he wasn't pumping, was working out the moves a jump ahead of his father and anxiously waiting to see if he was proved right or wrong. Meanwhile *Fathom* pitched reluctantly through the short seas, her old planks working and her seams weeping and the bilge water slapping up over the floorboards. Aaron swore at her as he pumped, crouching over the pump handle like a little wizened monkey.

One evening at dusk several of the smacks were running together before a fair wind half a mile off the mouth of the Marshfield creek. *Fathom* was leading. She was heavy-laden, and her boom was spread out wide to catch every breath of the mild wind. Tom was at the helm, Aaron was below, and Matt was on deck. They were all weary, for they had only had four or five hours' sleep the night before and had been away two days, but the wind was warm and there was the softness of spring in the air. Matt was sitting on the hatch cover looking out over the stern. *Charity* was not far behind them and looked likely to pass before they came to the creek. Her dark sails were goose-winged against the violet sky, her hull low to the water. Behind, strung out into the dusk, was the rest of the fleet. *Fathom* was proving yet again that, for all her antiquity, she was a fast boat. If she holds together, Matt was thinking, we might win the smacks' race in the regatta this summer. Last summer a split foresail had finished their chances.

He yawned and rubbed his eyes. At that same moment the wind veered. Tom was looking over his shoulder to see how *Charity* was doing, and the unexpectedness of the jibe took him off guard. As the boom came over, it struck him on the side of the head and knocked him straight over the transom into the water.

Matt sprung to his feet.

"Father!" he shouted.

Warding off the flailing sail, he leaped to the tiller and flung an arm out to his father. But already the tide had carried him well out of reach. With Aaron below and not likely in his witlessness to realize what was happening, Matt knew they stood no chance if he went into the water, too.

He wasn't a good swimmer—no better than his father.

"Aaron!" he shouted as he pushed the tiller over and feverishly gathered in the mainsheet. "Aaron, come up here!"

By the time the old man had come running up on deck Matt had got *Fathom* sailing again, reaching at right angles to her former course. He got her as close to the wind as she would go, but he knew it was impossible to sail straight back to where his father was floating in the water, for the wind was dead on the bows. It meant taking two tacks. Gritting his teeth, he turned her off on the first leg.

"The boom hit him, Aaron! Keep your eye on him. If we lose him once, we'll never find him again in this light!"

He could feel the sweat of fear on his hands. Already his father was only a vague blob on the water away off the starboard bow. How long he could keep up, Matt had no idea, even if he was conscious.

Not far away *Charity* was coming on with two crests of white foam curling back from her bows. Matt put *Fathom* about and set her on course for where he thought he could still see his father, although already it was difficult to be sure. But he could see that *Charity* would reach the spot before him.

Cupping his hand to his mouth, he shouted, "Mr. Beckett! My father has gone overboard! Look to your starboard bow!"

"I can't see him," Aaron muttered.

Matt bit his lip. "Mr. Beckett! My father's overboard!"

Matt jabbed his finger desperately as Beckett looked up. Matt knew Beckett must have heard him, but *Charity* was sailing on. She was right on the spot now where Matt thought his father was. Beckett was looking overboard, but even Matt now could see nothing in the water. *Fathom* was closing fast with *Charity*.

"He's gone," Aaron said.

Matt felt a lump of desperation in his throat. *Charity*'s sails were billowing across *Fathom*'s bows; she had not moved a degree off course. Matt was forced to give way and as he pushed the helm down he passed within feet of *Charity*'s skipper. Beckett said nothing. He was staring ahead, his face expressionless. As *Fathom*'s bows cleaved the froth of *Charity*'s wake Matt realized simultaneously two incredible truths: His father was drowned and Beckett hadn't lifted a finger to help him.

Matt turned *Fathom* up into the wind and stared at the shifting water. Not a thing moved. *Fathom*'s heavy sails flapped sullenly and her blocks tapped impatiently behind him, but he heard or felt nothing. It was as if his senses had left him. His father drowned . . . as Matt stared at the water he was still half expecting a hand to reach up for the transom, or to hear a shout. But the seconds went past and he saw and heard nothing, and when he put *Fathom* about again to search up and down, there was still nothing, only an interminable silence and an interminable area of sea. In the space of a few minutes his father had vanished, body and soul, off the face of the earth.

When the rest of the fleet came alongside to see what was wrong they found Matt at the helm with a face as white as chalk and old Aaron sitting on the hatch with tears running down his face.

"The boom hit him," Matt said. "He went overboard."

"Tom Pullen . . . the boom hit him." The word went through the fleet softly, voices were lowered, the smacks crowded together, jilling backwards and forwards round the stricken smack, and Matt was aware of a succession of faces passing by and repassing and the voices: "Tom Pullen is drowned. The boom hit him. . . ." "It's Tom Pullen—he's gone" until, still dazed, Matt saw George Firmin jump across onto *Fathom*'s deck.

He came and stood by Matt and said, "Come on. Take the old girl home. It's no good wasting time here."

Blindly Matt turned *Fathom* for the creek, shaking out the mainsheet, and the fleet spread out behind him and sailed silently home through the dusk.

The Money Belt

That night there were a lot of people in the Pullen cottage. Matt remembered his mother sobbing with her head in her arms and George standing there, red-faced, twisting his cap in his hands. Later, a friend of his mother's, a neighbor, made him drink a glass of brandy, although he thought it would burn his stomach up, and she took him upstairs and put him to bed as if he were ten years old. And although he was so weary and confused with the spirits, there was something lying on his conscience that would not let him sleep—and yet, somehow, with the brandy, he could not think exactly what it was. His mind was turning over like a steam engine, yet all his thoughts were meaningless. The baby was crying in the next room and there were neighbors' boots scraping the flags below, but within an hour Matt was asleep.

When he awoke the house was quiet. It was just getting light and through the square of the dormer window he could see a milky-blue sky, cloudless and calm. He looked at it for a long time without moving, and the thing that had been on his mind came to him clearly at last: He must find his father's body, for on it was the money that now was the family's only salvation. The money that, no doubt, had hastened his father's death, the weight of it dragging him down. Beyond that, Matt did not dare think.

He slid out of bed and pulled on his narrow stained trousers and dark jersey, and leaving his brothers still sleeping, he went downstairs and out into the morning. The dew drenched his bare feet as he walked down to the saltings. Redshanks and skylarks wheeled up from the mud. The tide was making, and way out to sea he could see a schooner heading for the London river, her topsails catching the sun. *Fathom* swung on her anchor, forlorn. Matt looked at her and an appalling feeling of loneliness flooded over him so that he had to fight back the tears. The face of the sea glittering in the sunlight beyond the saltings was as innocent and serene as he had ever seen it. The air was warm with the promise of summer, the grass shrill with the optimism of the skylarks. It was impossible to take in what had happened.

"Matt!"

He spun round blindly. George Firmin was coming down the track, leaving a trail in the dew.

"What are you about?" he asked gently as he came up. "I saw your track coming out of your cottage. Have you come to—to . . ." He hesitated.

"To look for him?" Matt said. "Yes. He had all that money in his belt. My mother will need it."

"Aye. No wonder he went down so quick. I remembered it afterwards. He showed it me that day he went round to Melville's to order the new smack." George stood looking over the saltings, considering. "The tide was making last night, when he went over," he said. "It had a couple of hours to go, too. He should come up on the saltings all right, unless the money keeps him down."

He glanced at Matt dubiously. The boy looked white and shaken.

"I'll find him, Matt. You bide here," he advised.

Matt shook his head. "No, I'll come with you. That's what I came down for."

George shrugged and they turned away from the hard onto the saltings. There were fresh footprints in the mud of the hard, coming up from the dinghies, and George remarked: "Looks as if someone else has been working early —or late."

Charity was lying astern of *Fathom* and *Miranda* off the hard, and the sight of her made Matt feel sick. He followed George in silence down onto the springy turf and they started to pick their way out to the shoreline. In some places the salting was quite firm; in others it was scored with deep winding creeks of soft mud which made a mazelike pattern across the surface. George had boots on and picked his way stolidly through while Matt rolled up his trousers and plunged on carelessly. At the shoreline they took separate ways and started to scour the myriad creeks and mudbanks that gave onto the sea, flushing up ducks and waders that flung themselves into the sky with a panic-stricken scurry of wings. The sun climbed higher and beat down warmly and the sea started to trickle into the saltings as the tide rose, filling the honeycombed ditches, until, two hours later, Matt and George were forced back to the sea wall. There, soaked and muddy, they flung themselves down on the warm turf.

"Not a sign," George said. "This tide might leave something, though. It's only a matter of time."

"I wouldn't care if it wasn't for the money," Matt said. "I don't mean that I don't care about my father, but a body— well, a body's not—not him, is it? I—I don't want to see him drowned."

"No. It's the money," George agreed. "You're going to need it," he added gently.

"Seventy-five sovereigns," Matt said.

"I know. The *Seaflower* money. He didn't bother to keep it secret. Everybody knew he had it in his belt."

"It's for the new smack," Matt said. "We must get it back because we'll never have the new boat without it."

George looked at Matt thoughtfully. "What are you going to do, Matt?" he asked gently. "Have you thought yet?"

Matt was staring out across the flooding saltings. George saw his jaw stiffen and a stubborn look came into his eyes.

"I shall do what my father did," he said quietly. "No one's going to turn me into a cheese merchant in Marchester. I shall get that money back and buy the *Reward* like we were going to, and when the twins are old enough they can come with me. It won't be long."

"Do you think your mother will let you—and that uncle of yours?"

"They'll have to," Matt said fiercely. "You did it, didn't you? Your father was drowned. You carried on with *Miranda*. Why shouldn't I?"

"I was eighteen," George said. "How old are you?"

"Sixteen," Matt said. "But what difference does that make? I've worked on *Fathom* since I was twelve."

George said quietly: "You've got quite a few mouths to feed. There's Aaron to keep, nets, rent, food. . . . And working *Fathom* with only two men is going to be hard work."

Matt looked at him angrily.

"I know all that," he said. "I thought about it when we were out on the mud over there, but it doesn't make any difference. What would you choose if you were me—cheese?" he asked bitterly.

"You might not get a choice. Your Uncle Albert seems to enjoy telling everyone what to do when he gets the chance."

George paused, and then looked at Matt rather awkwardly. "If there's anything I can do to help, Matt—I mean when all this is threshed out. If *Fathom* has to go, there would always be a place for you on *Miranda*."

"*Fathom* isn't going," Matt said stubbornly.

Even to George, his closest friend, he would not admit the fears he felt about the future. Although he had scarcely had time to think about it yet, he was already aware of the dreadful responsibilities that had fallen overnight on his shoulders. And, even worse than that, was the thought of Uncle Albert. George had had no need to remind him of Uncle Albert. The prospect was so fearful he turned his mind away from it. George, too, decided to change the subject.

"We'll search again at low water," he said. "I'll get my brothers down and we'll try the far side of the creek."

His eyes wandered thoughtfully across the water where the smacks were swinging now on the slack tide. Catching sight of *Charity*, he said suddenly, "Where was Beckett last night when your father went overboard? I thought he was up with you."

Matt said nothing for a few moments. If it had been anyone other than George asking the question, he would have held his tongue, but George's honest sympathy encouraged him to say what was on his mind.

"He *was* up with us," he said. "But he didn't choose to stop and help."

George looked at Matt curiously. "What do you mean?"

"He was nearer to my father than I was, just before he went down," Matt said. "I shouted to him, but he didn't even alter course, let alone luff up. He just kept on sailing."

George looked at Matt incredulously.

"He heard you? He knew what was happening?"

"If he's deaf, it's the first I've heard of it," Matt said. "I had to put my helm down to miss him, so you can tell how far away he was."

George whistled incredulously.

"What's he got against your father? It's scarcely possible!"

Matt shrugged. "There's the money, if that's anything." He paused. "Don't tell anyone what I've told you, George. I'd rather you didn't. My father's dead now. It makes no difference."

George shook his head angrily. "But it's incredible!" he murmured. "I remember thinking he must have been ahead of you, and not known what was happening. When we came in, I remember seeing *Charity* off the hard and no one on her. That's what made me think he must have been ahead, the fact that he'd had time to clear off before we even got into the creek."

Matt had no clear recollections of coming home the night before. He looked at *Charity* thoughtfully.

"Off the hard?" he repeated idly. "She's not off the hard now."

Fathom and *Miranda* were nearest to the hard. *Charity* was beyond *Miranda*. George looked at her absently.

"No," he said. Then he looked more closely and frowned. "No," he repeated. "That's strange. She was ahead of us when we put out the anchor last night."

"He must have come back and shifted her," Matt said. "I wonder why."

"Or—" George hesitated. Then he shrugged. "I don't know."

Matt did not pursue the subject. "I've been away long enough," he said. "I'd better get home. My mother will wonder where I've gone."

He got to his feet reluctantly. George stayed where he

was, his eyes brooding on *Charity*. He was obviously shaken
by what Matt had told him about Beckett. Matt hesitated.

"George, don't say anything about Beckett," he said again.
"I don't suppose he could have saved my father anyway."

George shook his head. "I won't say anything," he said.

Matt walked slowly home. It took quite an effort of will
power to go back. Once in at the door he knew that he must
start facing his problems. The whole family's problems were
his now, unless his mother preferred to look to her brother
for help. And as yet it was still hard even to realize that his
father was dead. The whole thing had happened so suddenly.
At the thought of life without his father Matt's brain became
numb. He could not even see himself as a person at all without his father, because up till now everything he had ever
done had been at his father's bidding. Matt felt as unpre-
pared to face what was in front of him as a naked bird that
had fallen out of its nest.

His mother was up and at the fire when he came in. She
was quite composed, although her eyes were red and her face
was pale. She had sent the twins off to school and Anne to
work as usual, and as Matt sat down at the table he had a
strange feeling that nothing had happened at all. His mother
glanced at his muddy legs and rolled-up trousers and guessed
what he had been out for.

"Did you find anything?" she asked as she set a bowl of
porridge down on the table before him.

Matt shook his head. "I'll go down at low water. George
is helping me."

"We shall need that money," she said.

"I know. We'll get it, don't worry."

She sat down at the table opposite him with a cup of tea
before her. "We shall have a hard time, Matt. I don't know
what to do for the best. I've sent word to Uncle Albert, but

I don't want to accept any help off him if I can help it. Tom wouldn't have wanted it. Not charity, you understand, only—"

She hesitated. Matt looked up swiftly. "Only what?"

"Only—if he were to offer you a place, that wouldn't be charity."

Matt said nothing. He could not trust himself to speak.

"Tell me what happened last night, Matt. It wasn't even a rough night. I never expected anything like that. If it had been the night you went out to the wreck—yes, but not this way."

Matt told her how the accident had happened.

"And was there no one close enough to pick him up before he went under? Was there no one behind you?" his mother asked.

"Beckett was right behind us, but—he—he wasn't quick enough," Matt said.

"Beckett?" Mary Pullen looked surprised. "I didn't think he came home with the fleet last night."

"Why not? He was up in front with us."

"I saw him come up the track at dawn. I thought he must have stayed out another tide." His mother took Matt's empty bowl and went back to the fire to refill it. Matt looked up in surprise.

"You saw him come up the track at dawn?" he said curiously. "Are you sure?"

"Yes, why?" She put the porridge on the table. "I couldn't sleep and Elizabeth was restless. I rocked her at the window, and I saw him walking up from the creek. There's no mistaking Beckett."

She did not pursue the subject, for there was only one thing on her mind at that moment. She sat staring into the dregs of her teacup, her face drawn and worried. Matt wanted to comfort her by saying that he would go and work for his Uncle Albert, but he could not get the words past his lips. They stuck in his throat like fishbones.

Presently some neighbors came in, and the vicar came down on his horse, and in the confusion Matt slipped out again and went back to the saltings. All afternoon he scoured the oozing creeks with George and his two brothers, and some more smacksmen worked from a dinghy on the far side of the creek, but nothing was found. Late in the afternoon, weary and disappointed, Matt met George again on the sea wall.

"Will you be fishing tomorrow, George?" he asked him.

"Aye, I'm trawling for soles."

Matt looked thoughtful, but he said nothing. They walked slowly back along the sea wall to the hard, and the sight of *Charity* again reminded him of the other thing that was on his mind.

"My mother said she saw Beckett come up the track at dawn," he said. "What do you make of that? Do you suppose he took *Charity* out again last night?"

George looked at Matt sharply. "He's a deep one, Beckett. Most of his work is done when there's no one else watching. I suppose he was up to some of his usual tricks, smuggling or some such. Unless—"

"Unless?" Matt queried.

He looked at George with a strange expression, wondering if George's faint suspicion was anything like his own. But George shook his head.

"Nothing," he said briefly.

The following morning a smacksman called Thomas discovered Tom Pullen's body on the shore as he was going out with the tide. But the belt with the money in it was missing.

Uncle Albert Calls

Matt did not hear the news until the evening, because the following day he took *Fathom* out trawling in company with George Firmin. Word had come that Uncle Albert would be riding over in the afternoon, and the moment he got wind of the message Matt made up his mind to take *Fathom* out. Then it would be quite plain what his intentions were. For he had no doubts about the plans in store for him, and the bitter struggle he was going to have to get his own way. He warned Aaron that *Fathom* would be going out on the tide early the next morning, and it was a comfort to him to find the old man waiting on the hard when he got down there. In the darkness—for it was barely three o'clock— several of the smacks were stirring. Matt was glad it was dark, for he didn't want any pitying glances and words of advice; he didn't want to have to explain his decision to anyone.

They rowed out to *Fathom* and in the darkness went about the routine preparations for setting sail. This was the worst part of all, going about the job that was so familiar and yet, at this particular moment, so utterly strange. Matt half expected to hear his father rating him for his clumsiness as he fumbled for the jib sheet. Nothing seemed to be in the right place. The gaff jammed and Matt almost sobbed as he coaxed it with the halyard. But somehow *Fathom* started sailing, the decks were tidied, the halyards coiled and the fair westerly freshened as the smacks reached out of the creek. Two hours later as the sun started to streak the sky over the marshes *Fathom* had her trawl out and was working with the rest of the fishing boats.

It was a strange day of contrasts for Matt, a day of warm heartening sunshine and fair winds, a day of sickening anxiety and uncertainty. Sometimes, as they trawled and the sun beat down on their backs and the sea fairly danced under *Fathom*'s bows, Matt couldn't help feeling faintly optimistic about the immediate future, but as soon as they were sweating to get the trawl in again and spilling its meager contents on the deck he felt hopelessly overwhelmed by what lay ahead of him. But he persevered and by the afternoon *Fathom* had a moderate catch, not one his father would have been very pleased about, but one which Matt felt did not disgrace him. At least it would mean some money to take home, as much as he'd ever earn at a day's cheese-paring in Marchester. When the tide turned, Aaron started to put away the trawl and Matt turned *Fathom* for home, beating into an afternoon sun that was turning the sea to fire. Half-closing his eyes against the melting brightness, he felt a few moments' weary satisfaction as he leaned on the tiller. The sun beat through his shirt, warm and comforting; even the wind was mild, chivvying a trail of gilt clouds across the horizon, and Matt wondered if this show of clemency was a good omen for him. At least it gave him courage, and he would need that when he got home.

In fact, he was to need it sooner than he knew. By the time *Fathom* got into the Marshfield creek she was in company with several more of the fleet. On the hard unloading was in full swing, laden rowing boats were laboring across the tide, voices were carrying on the wind down the water. Matt felt his nerves tingling at the thought of going home to face Uncle Albert, and he was in no hurry as *Fathom*'s anchor went overboard and he started to help Aaron load the catch into the dinghy. But as he handed down the first box he heard the splash of an oar close by, and looking up, he saw George sculling over from the hard. He straightened up as the boat came alongside, and knew from George's face that there was something wrong.

"What's the matter?" he asked.

"They've found your father, Matt, but there's no money on him."

Matt felt as if someone had punched him in the stomach. He stared at George blankly.

"No money on him?" he repeated.

"No money and no belt," George said. He put a hand up to hold his dinghy against *Fathom*. "He must have undone it to keep afloat," he added. "Unless the buckle broke."

Matt shook his head. He couldn't believe it. "That buckle would never break," he said. And somehow, in spite of the fact that it would have been the sensible thing to do, he couldn't see his father casting off that precious load. It had meant too much to him to be abandoned, even at the point of death. Even at the point of death? How could he ever be sure? Matt almost groaned.

"Who—who found him?"

"John Thomas. Amos was with him, too."

John Thomas was one of the most honest, God-fearing men in Marshfield. Matt could not imagine him taking the money. If Beckett had found it now . . .

"Does my mother know?"

"Yes, they told her."

Matt went on handing down the boxes to Aaron, his heart as heavy as lead. With the money gone, the outlook for the Pullen family was about as bleak as a mud flat in January.

"I'll take you ashore," George said as the last box was stowed. Matt nodded and stowed the sails while Aaron took the catch to the hard; then he got into George's dinghy and followed. He got the money for his catch and gave Aaron his share, but this first sign of independence gave him no pleasure.

"You didn't do so badly for your first day," George said, but Matt only shrugged.

"My Uncle Albert will be waiting up at the house," he said. "He'll have everything organized—what we're all to do, where we're all to go. What can I say now the money's gone? How can I keep the family by fishing *and* find seventy-five pounds before the year's out?"

"Melville won't press you for the money," George said. "He'll let you have the smack. And the money might turn up, Matt. We could try trawling for it at low water. He must have let it go, right at the end."

Matt gave George a doubtful look. "I suppose so," he said quietly.

"You did well today," George said as they walked slowly up the hill. "There was a few remarked on your spirit. They'll all stand by you, Matt, if you carry on. Don't let that grocer bully you."

But Matt did not feel very confident as he walked reluctantly up the garden path. He felt utterly discouraged and weary and all he longed for—as usual after twelve hours at sea—was a good meal in his stomach. But as soon as he pushed open the kitchen door he saw Uncle Albert sitting

before the fire in his father's chair. He had his legs stretched out and his clean white hands folded over his paunch, a glass of whisky on a little table beside him. His mother was sitting in her own chair, looking pale and rather nervous. The twins, extremely subdued, were sitting whispering together in a corner and Anne, just home from work, was eating her supper at the table. She looked up as Matt came in and her dark eyes spoke feelingly across the room, although she said not a word. Matt knew that at least he had an ally there.

His mother sprang up as he came in. "Oh, Matt, whatever did you go out for today? And without telling me? You knew your uncle was coming."

Although she sounded cross, Matt felt that it was more for Albert's benefit than his. Her eyes were not cross, and with her back to her brother, her face was tender and anxious.

Matt handed her the money, wishing it were six times as much.

"Well, it was worth-while," he said. "I've paid Aaron out of this."

He forced himself to cross the room and stand before his uncle.

"Good evening, Uncle."

Albert did not get up. He leaned forward and gave Matt a cold head-to-feet appraisal.

"At least I thought you would stay with your mother at a time like this, Matt. I don't consider your behavior very responsible. I've been waiting here for you since midday."

Matt thought, Well, you've certainly made yourself comfortable, but he bit his lip and said nothing. His mother came back to the fire and stirred the stew that was simmering there, but Albert did not take the hint. He had no intention of letting Matt escape in peace to the dinner table.

"We've been discussing the future, your mother and I," he said heavily, "and as it concerns you so vitally, as the eldest of the family, I think the least you could have done was to have put in an appearance."

"I was working," Matt said.

"Have you heard about your father?" his mother asked.

"That they've found him and the money is missing? Yes, George told me," Matt said.

"You realize, I suppose, what a very difficult situation you are all in, especially if the money is not found?" Albert pursued.

"Yes, I realize that," Matt said.

"Uncle Albert has suggested that we move to Marchester,

Matt," his mother said cautiously. "We could live over the shop and you boys could help your uncle."

From her voice and her expression, Matt could not tell whether she was for or against the idea. But he was too tired to waste time hedging.

"I won't come with you," he said steadily. "My father would have wanted me to go on working *Fathom*."

"Working *Fathom*!" his uncle snorted contemptuously. "A child like you! My dear boy, stop romancing. The idea is absurd."

Matt struggled to keep his temper in check.

"It isn't absurd," he said. "I've worked on her for nearly four years now. And the twins will soon be able to help me."

"But the boat is falling to pieces; you cannot deny it," Uncle Albert replied ruthlessly. "Do you really suppose that you, a mere boy, can earn enough to keep your family *and* buy a new boat within a year or two?"

His uncle's words were almost identical with the ones he had used to George himself not half an hour before, but coming from this quarter they goaded Matt.

"I'd rather die trying than work in your shop," he said defiantly.

His mother's hands went up to her face in dismay, and Uncle Albert launched himself out of his chair like an angry bull. His red face seemed to swell as he fumbled at his belt.

"By Heaven, I've always thought a good thrashing was just what you needed, my lad, and this is where you're going to get one!" he roared.

Matt took a step backwards and knocked the whisky bottle off the table with a crash. The cat, which had been lying by the fire, got up and fled between Uncle Albert's legs, almost knocking him flying, and Elizabeth, who had been asleep in her cradle, awoke with a startled yell. Matt's

one impulse was to get out of the house, but in the pande-
monium his mother leaped up and caught him by the arm.

"Stand still, Matt," she commanded. "And you, Albert, if
you lay a finger on this boy you'll never see nor hear from
us from this day forward!"

Her voice was so cutting that Albert stopped in midstride
and stared at her, panting heavily.

"Sit down!" she said. "Can't you see the boy is tired? It's
no time to start thrashing sense into him! Let him have his
meal and we'll talk sensibly."

"If he's tired, that's his fault," Uncle Albert snorted. "Insolent is what I'd call him—an insolent puppy! Always has
been. You've let him have his own way too long!"

But he did up his belt again and Matt's mother started to
ladle some stew out into a plate.

"Remember your manners, Matt," she said sharply as she
put it down on the table. "Sit down here now, and eat this."

Matt did as he was told, too tired to argue. The twins
watched him, their eyes round as marbles, and Anne gave
him another feeling look over the table. Beating or no, Matt
decided, nothing would induce him to go to Marchester,
even if the rest of the family went. His face was white and
stubborn as he ate his meal.

"If the boy had any sense, he would see I am trying to
help you all," Uncle Albert went on unctuously, having
settled himself back in Tom Pullen's chair.

"Yes, we all appreciate that," Mary Pullen said tactfully.
"But then you must remember that Tom made a good living
fishing and Matt won't always be a boy. His heart is on the
water, as Tom's was."

Matt was beginning to realize why Uncle Albert was so
gracious as to want them all under his roof in Marchester,
too. Albert was unmarried, and he paid a housekeeper to

run his home and cook for him. If his sister went to live with them, he could dispense with his housekeeper (and her wages) and put the rest of the family to work in his shop. In fact, they would all be unpaid assistants, working for their keep. He longed to point this out to his mother, in case she hadn't already thought of it, but didn't think it would be very wise at this moment.

Uncle Albert was saying, "But you must be practical, my dear Mary. There's that question of the new smack, now that the money appears to be missing. Even Tom never earned the money to buy one, not until he came by that reward. It's ridiculous to suppose that Matt could do so."

"It was Matt who earned the reward, you must remember," Mary Pullen said calmly. "He went aboard that wreck, not Tom."

"Besides, the money isn't lost yet," Matt put in. "We're trawling for it tomorrow."

"You cannot count on finding it," Albert snapped.

"Even without it," Matt said, "a quarter of the new smack is paid for. And Melville always lets smacksmen pay him when they're sailing." He spoke with more confidence than he felt. The dinner had put fresh heart into him.

Albert shot Matt a venomous glance and turned back to his sister.

"Well, it's for you to decide, Mary," he said stiffly. "If you decide to come to Marchester, the boy will have to come, too. He's only sixteen, a minor. He must do what you decide. I don't consider his attitude either helpful or co-operative, but then, it's only what I expected. Tom was always too soft with him."

He pulled out a gold watch and looked at the time.

"Six o'clock," he commented. "I am staying at the Plough and Sail tonight. I shall make the funeral arrangements in

the morning and see you later. Meanwhile you must make up your minds about the future."

He got up, smoothing down his waistcoat. He had a heavy red face decorated with carefully cultivated mutton-chop whiskers, and his dark eyes were small and shrewd. He dressed well, and the greatcoat his sister fetched him was beautifully tailored of expensive cloth. He adjusted the collar fastidiously and they all stood up as he took his leave. He kissed his sister coldly and then came and stood in front of Matt. Matt met his glance; he was already as tall as his uncle. His blue eyes were wary, but not afraid.

"As for you, Matt, think well. If you don't do as I wish, I shall not lift a finger to help you when you are in trouble."

Albert spoke softly, for Matt alone, and Matt said nothing. He clenched his hands. His uncle gave him a last cold glance and walked across to the door. Another moment and he had disappeared into the darkness.

"Oh! How I hate him!" Anne shouted, leaping up from the table.

"He's a monster!" Joe shouted.

"That will do!" said their mother sharply. "Get up to bed, Joe and Jack, and don't let me hear a murmur from you!"

Matt turned away from the table and sat on the edge of his father's chair, staring into the fire. Anne cleared away the dishes and Mary Pullen came and sat down again. Matt felt as if he had let his mother down, and met her glance uncertainly.

"Do you really want to go and live with him?" he asked.

"Not if you are set against it, Matt," his mother said. "It's the easy course to take, I suppose, but not much of a life for you boys, running errands in a shop. Not that it's any worse than fishing," she added bitterly. "When you and the twins are all working on the same boat, what shall I feel then, in the winter?"

"She'll be a good boat then, though," Matt said. "She won't founder. Not all smacksmen get drowned, Mother."

"They do if they keep at it long enough."

"But, Mother, if we go to him, he'll only make us all work for our board and keep. Then if we wanted to leave him, we wouldn't even have a home to go to. We'd be completely in his power. He only wants us for cheap labor—you, too, you know that."

"I'm afraid he's not a generous man," Mary Pullen agreed.

"If he really wanted to help us, he could easily enough. He's got plenty of money," Matt reflected. "Not that I'd like to take anything from him, but what he's doing really is blackmailing you. He's trying to force you to give up this cottage and live with him. He's not really offering to help *you*—it's himself he's helping. It would suit him fine to have us all working for him."

His mother sighed. "You're right, Matt, but it would be unwise to offend him. The twins are only eleven yet. You're going to have to work terribly hard to keep us all. We might be glad of a roof over our heads yet."

Matt was silent. His mother was right.

"I'll do what you want," he said, forcing the words out.

"Don't worry, Matt. We'll talk about it tomorrow. You must be tired to death. I don't know what to do for the best either."

She drew him some hot water from the fire and he went out into the scullery and washed. Later when he went up to bed Anne was in her nightdress at the top of the stairs. Anne was fourteen, a tall eager girl who could not imagine life among the smells of Marchester.

"D'you think I'd be any good on a smack?" she asked as he came up. "I've got great big arms with scrubbing those vicarage flags. I'd help you."

Matt smiled. "You'd frighten the fish for miles," he said.

Anne looked at him gravely. "We won't go to Marchester, though, Matt, whatever happens, will we?"

"I hope not," he said. It was all the encouragement he could find to give her.

The next day *Fathom* and *Miranda* and two more smacks trawled for the money belt, but nothing was found. It was a heartbreaking business, for they all knew that they might miss the thing by inches—or by miles. Although Matt had steeled himself to expect nothing, he felt bitterly disappointed after a day's fruitless search.

The next day Tom Pullen was buried in the churchyard on the top of the hill. Nearly all the smacksmen attended, garbed in their Sunday black, solemn and silent as they stood round the grave. Away down the hill, beyond the newly green elms, the creek and the estuary basked innocently in the sun. Only the number of smacks on their mooring told that something was amiss. Way out, a solitary sail could be seen trawling off the shoals. Matt guessed it was *Charity,* for Beckett was not among the mourners. Perhaps, Matt thought, Beckett knew that not many would stay at home to see him buried if he were drowned, and he was not going to join the churchgoers for the sake of convention. Most of the fishermen were accustomed to periodic visits to the churchyard for the sake of paying their last respects to one of their fellows, but more often it was in the wintertime, when the wind howled in the elms, remnants of the very gale that, most likely, had brought about the sad event. The modest headstones all told a similar tale: "Drowned at Sea, 1872." "Lost from the smack *Emma*, aged 16," "Lost in the Swin" . . . "Drowned" . . . "Drowned" . . . Matt, in spite of the evidence that had surrounded him all his life, had never supposed that tragedy might come to his own family in this way. Now, brought face to face with it by the sight of his father's coffin disappearing into the earth, he felt that he was dreaming and that soon he would wake up to the sound of his father's voice hurrying him out of bed. But no such relief was forthcoming, and as the truth of the fact sunk in, that his father was drowned and he would never see him again, his grief rose up and overwhelmed him.

After the funeral some of Tom's relatives, Uncle Albert, and some of the family's close friends went back to the Pullen home for lunch while the smacksmen went home to change and then down to the creek to catch the next tide.

As George Firmin went down the track he paused at the gate. Anne Pullen was emptying some scraps from the table into the hen pen and when he saw her George said, "Is Matt in there, Anne? I'd like a word with him if he's not busy."

Anne nodded and went inside, and the next minute Matt was at the gate, glad of the opportunity to get away from the company for a brief spell.

"Can you spare a minute, Matt?" George asked. "Maybe I shouldn't say what I'm going to say—not at this moment— but I've thought about it so long I've got to come out with it. It's about that money belt."

Matt looked at him sharply. "Does it concern Beckett, too?" he asked quietly.

George nodded. "Aye. I might have guessed you'd have been on to it, too."

"He knew about the money belt all right," Matt said. "None had better cause to know about it than him. And why did he take *Charity* out again that night? To look at the stars?"

"I wouldn't have said anything, Matt—because we can never prove it—but my mother said something just now that set me thinking again. You know how these women gossip. Beckett's wife has learned to hold her tongue for fear of her husband, but she can't help bragging like the rest of 'em. She told my mother her men are buying another smack, a new one. I reckon there's nothing remarkable in that, considering there's four of 'em, but it's just that it set me thinking again. The timing might be a coincidence but . . . well, I've thought about it so long I can't keep quiet about it any longer. You know what's in my mind well enough."

Matt stared bitterly at George. "Yes, it's no more than what I think myself," he said softly. "There's nothing

Beckett would stop at, not even thieving from the dead. My father never loosed that buckle, I swear it. Yes, I've thought about it, but what good did it do me? How could we ever accuse him of it? There's not a shred of evidence."

"No, you'd be a fool to accuse him. He's a dangerous man. But we'll bear it in mind, Matt. Perhaps we're wrong—perhaps we're not. Perhaps I shouldn't have told you this, but—well, it's been in my head and I guessed you'd have wondered about it, too. It'll go no farther."

"No. Not even to my mother."

"It wouldn't pay you to cross Beckett, Matt. Remember that."

"No. I know." Matt was only too well aware of his vulnerability. Since his father's death he was as puny and helpless as a shrimp in a dish against such adversaries as Beckett and Uncle Albert. It was going to be all he could do to exist in the future, let alone take on enemies of Beckett's caliber.

"I'm glad you told me," he said.

George said, "I must go, or my brothers will be waiting. Will you be fishing tomorrow, Matt?"

Matt hesitated. "I—yes. Yes, I'll be coming," he said.

George walked on down the track and Matt stood looking after him, his face drawn and pale. George's words had come as no surprise to him, but he could not help feeling very bitter at this verification of his suspicions. That the money was lost was bad enough, but lost to Beckett . . . ! Yet what could he do about it? There was nothing. George knew it too. Matt stared down the hill to where the sails were going up beyond the sea wall, and in that moment decided, whatever happened, he would carry on fishing. He longed to walk out of the gate, then and there, and follow George down to the hard, but knew that he must see the day through at home. And tell Uncle Albert. If his mother still wanted to go to Marchester, she would have to go without him.

He went back into the house. His father's cousins were chatting round the table. Uncle Albert was putting on his coat and Matt's mother was standing beside him nervously. When Matt came in she gave him a worried look and said, "Uncle Albert is going now, Matt. He wants to know what you're going to do."

"I'm going to work *Fathom*, Mother," Matt said.

"Even without the money?"

Matt nodded. "Yes. If you want to go to Marchester, I'll stay here alone. I can sleep at George's."

"There's no question of that," his mother said. "If you stay, we all stay."

It would have helped Matt if she had looked pleased at his initiative, but she suddenly looked very old. She did not look proud of him either; she did not look angry. She merely looked very tired.

"In that case," Uncle Albert said, pulling up his collar, "I'll wish you good day."

His nostrils were dilated with anger. His little beady eyes glittered at the insult Matt had dealt him. Matt suddenly thought that he looked like the old cockerel outside in the hen pen, swollen with ridiculous self-importance. But the idea didn't really comfort him much as his uncle stalked away down the path and out of sight. It was only when his uncle had gone that he realized just how it felt to be the sole supporter of a family of five.

A Schooner in the Fog

Matt put his head out of the hatch and peered into the darkness. *Fathom*'s port and starboard lights burned steadily in the shrouds only a few yards off, yet the light was nebulous and dim, swimming out of dense fog. *Fathom* lay motionless, silent, drops of moisture beading every spar, her sails in a useless bundle on deck.

"It's still the same," Matt said. The wet air was like cobwebs on his face, the stillness unreal and nerve-wracking. He spoke to Aaron, as usual, but as usual he got no reply. After twelve hours at anchor in this blind white fog, Matt felt the inaction and uncertainty getting on his nerves. Pausing in the hatchway, he thought he would scream if he had to spend another hour in the stuffy fo'c'sle with the mumbling old man.

They had been making for home when the fog had crept up out of a strange hazy afternoon. For a time they had felt their way along with the lead, but when the wind had died on them completely he had put his anchor out before the tide should carry them aground, for there were shoals all round them. *Fathom* was too old a craft to risk grounding now. The shoals here were of sand, as hard as iron. Since then he had seen or heard nothing, although he was on the edge of the passage through from the Thames up the East Coast. He knew he wouldn't be the only one benighted and at anchor, waiting anxiously for the first sign of wind.

He felt desperately tired, but he hadn't slept much below; he was too anxious to be moving again. Fog made his flesh creep. It was like being wrapped in cotton wool, blind and muffled and senseless, and the small sounds of the idle boat, the dripping from the spars, the tapping of a block, the occasional grating of the anchor chain, irritated him beyond measure. The cuddy below was dim with smoke from the ancient stove, and as thick and unpleasant as the atmosphere above. Matt gave an impatient sigh and wiped the moisture from his forelock.

"It's no better," he said as he went below again. "Let's hope it will shift when dawn comes."

It was then not long after midnight, and Matt followed Aaron's example by rolling into his bunk and trying to get some sleep. But just when he most needed it, sleep would not come quickly. For all his weariness this last month since his father had been drowned, he was getting used to these dreaded hours when sleep eluded him, and the specter of his own frailty haunted him instead. Sometimes he found himself thinking of Uncle Albert's shop not as a martyrdom but as a haven, a sanctuary from the inexorable tides and the responsibility of wresting a living from them. And this treachery of the imagination in turn was a worse torment than physical exhaustion. His pride could not stomach it. He would force his thoughts away and start wondering how it was that his father had always found a catch so quickly and filled his hold so consistently. He realized only too well that he had never appreciated his father's skill; he had taken the full hold for granted. Only these last weeks, wracked with the effort of making half his father's catches in twice the time, did he realize that his four years of sea time was a pathetic apprenticeship for the task he had taken on. Matt turned in his bunk with a sigh that was almost a groan. Sleep, when it came, was like drowning in a black pit.

He was awakened by *Fathom*'s pitching. For a moment he lay listening. The halyards were slapping on the mast and the anchor chain was snubbing. The sounds were like music in his ears. He got up and stumbled up the companionway. As he put his head out a cold breeze fanned his cheek and his hair blew up from his forehead. It was still pitch-dark and the visibility was very bad, but Matt knew that good weather was on the way. In a space of seconds his spirits lifted. He put his head back into the hatch and shouted. "Aaron! The wind has come!"

By the time the old man had come muttering up on deck, Matt had the mainsail up and was bringing in the anchor. He knew it might have been wiser to wait until dawn, but he had had his fill of sitting about and he felt that he knew his whereabouts well enough to feel his way along the edge of the channel. By the time dawn was breaking he would be well inshore.

The fog was patchy now. As *Fathom* sailed, a light fluky wind on her beam, it cleared and thickened alternately. Matt stood at the tiller, his eyes on the compass, and Aaron stood up in the bows with the lead swinging methodically. They had only been going about five minutes when Aaron let out a strangled shout from forward. Matt glanced up and saw a red light looming out of the darkness way above his head, so close that his heart stopped beating. Instantly he put the tiller over and braced himself for the jibe.

"Hold on, Aaron!"

Fathom went about with a crashing of sails, her boom slamming over with a wrench that brought Matt out in a

cold sweat. High above her straining sails, Matt saw the ghost of a ship bearing down on them, a bowspritful of sails like white teeth gnashing at them out of the darkness. For a moment he thought *Fathom* would be smashed to pulp. He heard a startled shout from the deck above and, looking up, saw the great bowsprit miss *Fathom*'s mast by inches. *Fathom* wallowed as the big ship took her wind, and Matt could have touched the towering hull from where he stood as it slipped past. But the moment he saw that *Fathom* was out of danger, his blood ran cold at the schooner's folly.

Cupping his hands round his mouth, he yelled with all his might: "Ahoy there! Heave to, or you will run aground!"

The wind filled *Fathom*'s sails again and he put her about quickly after the big ship. It was a three-masted schooner, a foreigner by her flag, and certainly with no idea of her position. Whether anyone on deck would either hear or understand his shouting he could not tell, but he went on shouting after her: "Heave to! You are running into danger!"

He heard men running along her decks and a frenzied gabble of conversation. The fog had cleared, but it was still dark and he could not see what was going on. He could only see the vague shape of the sails ahead of him. At any moment he expected to hear frantic shouts as she grounded, and the seconds after he lost sight of her were pregnant with anxiety. A deep-keeled schooner such as she could not afford to go aground on an ebbing tide. Matt knew she would fall over and sink immediately, as many had done before her on this treacherous coast.

But in a minute he realized that his warning had been heeded. The schooner was lying up into the wind and her crew were taking the headsails off her. He heard the urgent rattle of the anchor running out and a voice shouted:

"Who is there? The captain wants speak you."

Matt sailed *Fathom* close alongside the now stationary schooner. A row of white faces were peering over the rail above him, and the foreign voice went on:

"Will you send the man up? The captain wants speak you."

There was a shouted order and a rope was slung down over the ship's side. Matt put *Fathom* about, his mind racing. It was obvious that the schooner was lost and had no pilot aboard. If he took on the job, he could expect some money from it; he would also be taking responsibility for a ship of some hundred tons and God knew how many lives. It was the sort of opportunity that came a smacksman's way once in a lifetime, but Matt's stomach shrunk into a cold knot of apprehension at the thought of tackling it.

"Aaron," he said, and paused. What was the use? The fog was clearing. There was about another hour to go to dawn. By then, if the schooner waited, she could no doubt find another pilot. The opportunity would never come again. Matt's eyes went to the dangling rope. Aaron stood beside him, muttering excitedly.

The commanding foreign voice called down again from the schooner's deck: "May we have the man aboard, please? The captain ask you."

Matt turned to Aaron. "Run her alongside, Aaron. I'll go and see what they want. They might be all right if I just show them their position."

Aaron took the tiller and sailed *Fathom* to windward of the schooner, where she reached in neatly under the schooner's hull. Matt went forward and strained his eyes into the darkness, but a judicious throw of a rope from above solved his anxiety. It landed right beside him; he grasped it simultaneously and swarmed up the smooth hull to land over the rail among the staring crew. The man whom Matt gathered had issued the invitation came forward, and a pair of doubtful eyes looked him up and down.

"Are you the man in charge of the fishing boat?" he asked with obvious disbelief.

"Yes, sir," Matt said firmly.

"You know your position?"

"Yes, sir." He would have liked to add, "Of course," but

decided that it would be tactless. The mate's scornful eyes nettled him.

"You come and see the captain, please," he ordered, and the sailors stood back as the two of them marched aft. The deck was a mass of hastily struck sails, and from the main companionway faces were peering; a group of people that Matt took to be passengers stood muttering, staring at him curiously as he went past. From the language Matt thought the ship was Dutch, but since he was no linguist, he couldn't be sure.

The captain stood by the helm. A vast man with a face like a bulldog and shrewd angry eyes, he looked at Matt searchingly as he stepped into the smoking lantern-light. Matt blinked and tried to fight down a sick feeling of nervousness. The mate spoke rapidly to the captain in his own language, and the captain snapped something back. The mate said to Matt:

"He ask you if you know your position, and are you the captain of the fishing boat or the boy?"

Having accepted Matt's reply a minute earlier, he looked slightly apologetic at having to repeat the questions, and nodded appeasingly as Matt said, "Yes, sir. I know the position and the smack is mine."

The captain nodded curtly and shouted at a sailor, who stepped forward with a chart. He indicated to Matt to point to their position, and Matt—who had never seen a chart in his life before—had to deliberate carefully before he was able to put his finger on a spot on the north edge of the Buxey sands.

The captain immediately rolled his eyes and broke into a torrent of angry abuse at everyone around him. The mate turned pale, the man with the chart crossed himself, and in

the commotion Matt was relieved to hear a very English voice say, "What is going on here? Are we aground?"

The mate stepped back respectfully as a tall, well-dressed man of about fifty came forward. He seemed to be a man of authority, for even the captain stopped cursing. He spoke sharply to the mate again, and the mate explained the situation:

"The boy say we are in danger of going aground, sir. He shout at us from the smack."

The man turned to Matt and said coolly, "Is that so? Where are we?"

"On the north edge of the Buxey sands, sir," Matt replied. Again he pointed it out on the chart.

The Englishman clicked his tongue against his teeth and said mildly, "My God."

At this point another figure came into the circle of light cast by the lantern over the chart. Matt looked up and saw a boy of about his own age, with fine features, dark eyes, and reddish-brown hair. He was dressed in dark, expensive clothes and, by the resemblance, was obviously the son of the older man. He was also, Matt immediately realized, the boy he had met the summer before, the boy from the *Good Fortune.*

"What's the matter, Father?"

"We're in among the shoals, my boy, halfway up a sandbank, according to this boy here."

The boy looked up and his eyes met Matt's. Immediately they lit up with recognition.

"Why, it's you! Matt—Matt Pullen. Father, this is the boy I told you about last summer, when that painter fell overboard. Do you remember? He pulled us both out. This is my father, Matt, Mr. Shelley."

Mr. Shelley gave Matt a thoughtful scrutiny and held out his hand. "I'm glad to meet you. Doubly so, if you know where we are. Could you pilot us into deep water?"

"Yes, sir."

Mr. Shelley turned to the mate and the captain. "I suggest you let this boy take the ship into deep water."

"*Ja, ja.*" The captain nodded, and a look of relief flashed over the mate's face.

"We're supposed to be going into the Thames," Mr. Shelley elaborated. Matt had already guessed that.

"I think we had better move quickly, sir," he said. "The tide is ebbing."

All the while he had been standing there he had half expected to feel the big ship tremble as the tide ebbed from under her keel. The moment his words were translated to the captain he was relieved to see the crew leap into action. The mate started to bark out orders, sailors dispersed at the run to sheets and winches, and sails six times as big as *Fathom*'s began to go aloft, flapping sullenly along the luffs with impatience. The schooner stirred and swung and the windlass groaned from the bows. Matt watched the movement eagerly, staring as the white canvas blossomed over his head and the sailors swung on the halyards, cursing and sweating. The wind was light, the sky still as dark as pitch, although Matt knew dawn could not be far away. All his life he had wanted to go aboard a big ship, but it had never occurred to him in his wildest dreams that he would go aboard one as a pilot. His mind now was a confused mixture of excitement and apprehension as he stood beside the helmsman, the formidable captain in silence behind him. He felt the pulse beating in his throat. The mate came back and reported to the captain, who made an impatient gesture. The mate turned uncertainly to Matt.

"She is ready to sail," he said.

"Tell me what she draws," Matt said steadily.

The mate quoted a figure in meters which meant nothing to Matt, but Mr. Shelley stepped forward and said, "Three meters. That will be ten feet."

Matt nodded.

"She must pay off to starboard," he said. "The shoal is under her port bow. Then the course is northeast by east, and keep the leadline going on the starboard bow."

The mate turned and barked out more orders. The windlass creaked, sheets were let out, and as the anchor broke out the schooner paid off as sweetly as *Fathom* herself, slipping silently into the darkness, her sails drawing with a gentle creaking overhead. As soon as she had way on, the mate gave the order to put her about and once more there was a scurry to the sheets, the great sails slatted over, and the ship heeled away on her new course, tumbling the water across her bows.

"We throw a line to your boat, she follow us," the mate reported to Matt, when all sheets were made fast again. Matt, who had completely forgotten Aaron, nodded absently. If the schooner ran clear now, she would be out of danger. He stood listening to the calls of the leadsman up on the bow, which the mate translated to him, his eyes on the compass needle flickering in the binnacle light.

Attracted by the commotion on deck, most of the passengers seemed to have come up to take stock of the situation. From a glance at their appearance Matt got the impression that they were passengers of some importance. A small group of them came up to talk to Mr. Shelley, but Matt could not understand any of their conversation; he only gathered that they were worried about something. They passed on from the Englishman to the captain, and Matt heard what sounded like an altercation going on behind him. The captain sounded very angry, but the passengers seemed to carry weight. He beckoned to Mr. Shelley. Another conference took place, and in a few minutes Mr. Shelley was at Matt's elbow.

"The Dutch gentlemen want to know how long this mistake is going to cost us. They are very disturbed at the delay," he said. "I am afraid they have too much influence with the captain. It is because of them that the ship sailed before the fog dispersed."

Matt looked up. "It means going back round the Gunfleet to get into the Swin, sir," he said.

Mr. Shelley stared at the chart for several seconds to work this out.

"That's quite a few miles," he said. "Are there no short cuts?"

Matt looked up in surprise. It hadn't occurred to him to take short cuts in a vessel the size of this.

"There's the Spitway, sir. The smacks all use it. But they don't draw ten feet."

"You mean it's not deep enough?"

Matt thought rapidly. "What time is it?" he asked.

Mr. Shelley consulted a gold watch at his waist.

"Almost four o'clock," he said.

"She would do it," Matt said. "The tide is on the ebb, though. It's not wise."

He felt rather worried as Mr. Shelley turned away and started talking in Dutch again behind him. Surely they weren't going to ask him to take the schooner through the Spitway two hours before low water? The Spitway was a channel between the long and otherwise continuous Buxey and Gunfleet sands, between them stretching about sixteen miles in a northeasterly direction four miles offshore. The sands dried out completely at low water, but the Spitway was generally covered with about eight feet of water at the lowest state of the tide. Shoal-draught vessels like smacks and barges used it regularly, but Matt doubted if a schooner with ten feet under her had ever attempted it two hours before low water. He knew he was right when he said it was possible, but whether he could locate the channel and get through it in time, before the tide ebbed too far, was another matter. The channel was a bare quarter of a mile wide, and every minute as the water ebbed would see the margin of error grow less. He glanced over his shoulder to see the captain and mate in conference over the chart and the cold weight of his responsibilities began to press on him.

In a minute the mate was at his side.

"The captain asks you if you can find your way through the Spitway," he said.

"Yes, sir. I could."

"She will go through?"

"Yes, sir. But it would be very dangerous at this state of the tide."

The mate went back to the captain and apparently reported Matt's opinions. The Dutch gentlemen, who had been listening, joined in the conversation, and what appeared to be a heated argument ensued. Francis's father stood by, taking it all in. Then he moved over to Matt and explained the situation.

"These Dutchmen are diamond merchants," he said. "They are sailing to London to attend an auction this afternoon. Now that the ship has been delayed they are worried about getting there in time. In fact, they obviously prefer to drown us all than miss bidding for their stones. I think you'll find, after they have offered the captain enough money, that you will be asked to take the ship through the Spitway. Do you think you can?"

"Yes, sir. But she'll be very close to the bottom. If the wind fails, she'll go aground."

"Of course, you could refuse."

Matt looked up, his face tense. Mr. Shelley was looking at him searchingly.

"Will they offer me enough money, too?" he asked bluntly.

A month ago the words would never have come into his head, let alone have passed his lips. He was honest enough not to be ashamed of them either, although Mr. Shelley looked surprised. His eyes narrowed and he shrugged rather contemptuously.

"I've no doubt you'll get what you ask," he said coolly.

Matt flushed in the darkness, but his resolution did not change. What did Mr. Peregrine Shelley know of shrimping for the family's bread? His tiepin alone would have kept the Pullen family for a month.

The mate stepped forward and said to Matt, "You are to go through the Spitway."

"Yes, sir."

Matt clenched his hands and stared fiercely at the compass. For a moment his head reeled at the responsibility he had taken on. Only an hour ago he had been fast asleep on *Fathom*; now he was master of a schooner with a crew at the ready to obey his orders and half the merchants of Holland watching him like hawks beyond the helm. But instead of feeling proud and heady at this sudden acquisition of power, he had only to raise his eyes to those taut sails above his head and listen to the kiss and slap of the water under those fast clipper bows to feel appalled at what he had to do. He set his jaw to stop his lip from trembling and kept his eyes on the compass, praying for his confidence to come back. The mate was at his elbow, pale and miserable, and Mr. Shelley, his eyes grave, had withdrawn slightly and stood staring into the darkness. Francis stood with him, watching Matt.

"Due east," Matt said to the mate. "Keep the leadline going, and translate for me. We shall have to find the channel by the soundings."

The mate gave his orders. The helmsman hauled on the wheel, and the schooner's bows swung round towards the shoals once more. The wind was freshening and Matt would have preferred to have some canvas off her, to give him more time to deliberate, but the sooner they got through the Spitway the more water there would be in it, and he knew he would be a fool to reef. He would just have to think quickly and pray that the callings were accurate.

"Three fathoms and a half," the mate translated.

Matt stared at the great pulling sails, waiting. The sky was still dark, although the fog had lifted. A few stars shone dimly above the foremast.

"Three fathoms."

Matt could smell cigar smoke and hear the captain grumbling behind him. He fastened his eyes on the flickering compass needle again.

"Two and three-quarter fathoms."

The chant of the man on the leadline made the situation apparent to the most ignorant of the onlookers. The Dutch merchants stood in silence, their eyes pondering doubtfully on the boy at the helmsman's elbows. His face was expressionless in the binnacle light.

"Two and a half fathoms."

Matt changed the course by a few degrees. There was nothing in his head now but the pattern of the shoals beneath them. He was feeling a way along the edge of the sand, waiting for the deepening that would show him the presence of the channel. He was completely involved in his task now, oblivious to the tension around him. The call came again.

"Two and a half fathoms."

The schooner slipped on, her wake shining behind her. The mate's face was glistening with sweat. At the next call, he looked up sharply.

"Two and a quarter fathoms."

Matt hesitated.

"Two and a quarter fathoms," the mate repeated urgently.

Matt decided to hold his course. He nodded, but said nothing. It seemed hours before the next call came, and then it was constant.

"Two and a quarter fathoms."

Matt nodded again. The schooner was so strong, he was thinking, her sails creaking and stretching all round him. The task was so delicate: A few inches of water could mean life or death to her, yet she flung on eagerly through the darkness, tossing up her bow wave. The seconds spun out again before the leadsman called, and Matt felt the fear building up inside him.

"Two and a quarter fathoms."

The mate looked at Matt almost appealingly. But Matt was not to be moved. He said nothing, and the helmsman kept his hands steady on the wheel, although the sweat of fear was running down his face. The leadsman swung and called and the mate translated.

"Two and a quarter fathoms."

The first pale suggestion of dawn was lightening the sky behind them, but over the bows the night was like black velvet, thick and blind. Somewhere beyond, Matt knew, the Gunfleet would be slowly revealing herself; in the dawn her sands would shine innocently, the birds playing along the edge and rising up with shrill piping cries. He had seen it a thousand times, and counted the wrecks with his father, some fresh and stark, others half-buried skeletons that had sailed a century ago.

"Two and a quarter fathoms," the mate said." *Mijn God,* how long we go like this?" he added.

Matt did not answer. The next cry came, and Matt recognized a difference.

"Two and a half fathoms," the mate said excitedly.

It might be the channel, or it might just be an indentation in the sands. Matt waited.

"Three fathoms."

"Southeast by east," Matt said.

The mate bawled out orders and the crew leaped to trim the sheets as the schooner changed course. The wind was almost dead aft now and the mate eyed the sails anxiously.

"Three fathoms."

Everyone was looking much happier suddenly, as if the danger were over, but Matt knew that it was only just beginning. The Spitway would go shallower than three fathoms before they were through. If Mr. Shelley's watch was wrong, the water might already be too shallow. And if it wasn't the Spitway . . . Matt's nerves tightened at the thought. His heart was thudding in his breast with a terrible apprehension as the schooner slipped on, brushing a few paling stars with her mast tops.

"Three fathoms."

The calls seemed a century apart.

"Two and three-quarter fathoms."

"Two and a half fathoms."

The schooner sailed on like a gliding gull. Everyone aboard her was tense and silent. Only the leadsman's voice came at intervals and the anxious repetition of the mate to Matt, and Matt nodded and said nothing. Call by call the water was ebbing off the sands.

"Two and a quarter fathoms."

"Two and a quarter fathoms."

"Two fathoms."

The mate's face was green and the sweat rolled in great drops off his nose. Matt stood motionless, waiting. He had the consolation of knowing, at least, that the ship was in the

Spitway, else she would have gone aground already, but his body was tensed for the jar of the keel on the sand. He could see it below him, the heel kissing the smooth sand, the little inches of water between them, and all the power of the fresh wind in the sails above, pulling the schooner on as if a hundred fathoms of ocean rolled beneath them. The pearl-gray streamers of dawn were raggedly filling the sky, but if the light came to show them their mistake, it would be too late. Matt could feel Mr. Shelley's eyes resting on him, but he was not afraid of the decision he had made. If the schooner touched, the blame would be his, but he had not made his decision in ignorance.

"Two fathoms."

Francis said to his father in a low voice, "Do you think she'll go, Father?"

Mr. Shelley shrugged. "Your friend's not panicking," he said softly.

"Two fathoms."

The mate almost groaned as he repeated the stubborn figure. Matt was straining his ears for an echo of the Swin Spitway buoy which tolled on the far side of the channel. He thought he had heard it already, its sad restless note booming across the water, but he said nothing.

"Two and a quarter fathoms!"

Matt sensed the excitement in the leadsman's call before the mate repeated it. His expression did not change, but he felt as if a weight had lifted off his thumping heart.

"Two and a half fathoms!"

The mate turned to Matt, his sweating face breaking into an almost comical relief.

"She is through?" he stammered.

"Yes. Listen, there's the buoy." The sound of the bell came

quite clearly now, fitful and sad from its eternal tether on the shoals.

"Look." Matt nodded to port, staring into the gray distance. The first faint gleam of sunlight was stealing across the water, and in its path a strange gleaming shadow rose up out of the water, waves breaking along the edge to sparkle in the light. It was the edge of the Gunfleet, uncovering in the ebb.

The mate shuddered. "Terrible, terrible," he muttered. Then he turned away to speak to the captain, who had been standing all this time in a state of frozen horror behind the helmsman. His bulldog face looked a good ten years older than an hour before, although it was creasing now into a grim smile. As the mate spoke to him, he put up a trembling hand to tug at his collar, rolling his eyes with relief.

"*Ja, ja,*" he kept saying. "*Goed, goed.*"

"When we have passed the buoy she can go about and make a southwesterly course for the Whitaker, sir," Matt said. "That will see her into the Swin and in an hour she will have a fair tide into the Thames."

He stepped back, turning away from the compass, feeling suddenly so cold and tired he thought he would fall over where he stood. His hands shook, and he plunged them into his pockets.

Mr. Shelley stepped forward. "I suggest you come down to my cabin for a drink before you leave us," he said briskly. "We could all do with one."

It was more an order than an invitation, and Matt found himself following Mr. Shelley dumbly along the deck. Everyone stared at him as he went past, for what he had done was now apparent to everyone on board the ship. In the spreading light of dawn the breakers of both the Buxey and the Gunfleet banks were shining white astern, one to port and the other to starboard, grim evidence of the dangers the schooner had so narrowly escaped. Mr. Shelley paused to survey the scene at the top of the companionway, and he shook his head slowly as he took it in: the shining scene of sand and sea, so apparently innocent, so utterly treacherous; the landscape that was home to Matt.

Then he straightened up and said briskly once more, "Come, my boy. Follow me."

A Hand for the *Good Fortune*

Matt knew he ought to get back on *Fathom* and make for home, but he hadn't the will to refuse Mr. Shelley's invitation. He felt limp and exhausted, his mind a blank. He followed Shelley and his son along a narrow corridor and in a few moments found himself in a neat cabin, all done out in mahogany with carpets, draperies, mirrors, and gilt work. A stove was burning, a steward hovered to take orders. Matt sank down in the armchair indicated and made an effort to pull himself together. He was shivering and, after the intense concentration of the last hour, his mind was now confused and weary. In this suddenly civilized setting he felt as out of place as a fish in a field, conscious of his fish-reeking clothes and black, calloused hands.

But if Mr. Shelley had been somewhat distant earlier, he was now full of concern to make Matt comfortable. The steward brought a steaming silver jug of coffee, and poured out a strong brew for Matt, which the boy took gratefully. The stuff went down him like fire and he realized that he hadn't had anything inside him save a few shrimps for the last twelve hours. What a night! After *Fathom*'s miserable cuddy this cabin was as opulent as a drawing room. Matt, glancing round, saw Francis watching him from the plush-covered bunk, and he remembered the time he had watched him from the bows of the *Good Fortune*. The reddish-brown eyes gave very little away, and Matt was not to know that Francis was once again full of admiration and envy for Matt's familiarity with the ways of sailing. Francis's father,

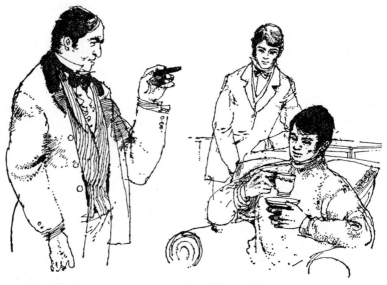

lighting up a cigar, studied him thoughtfully through the fragrant haze.

"You're very young to have your own smack," he remarked.

"Yes, sir," Matt said. He paused, and knew that the remark was really a question. "My father was drowned a month ago," he explained. "Before then I worked on it with him. Now there is just me and Aaron—he's a good hand, but his mind has gone."

Shelley's eyebrows went up. "A boy and an imbecile," he murmured. "Can you make a living?"

Matt, rather stung by the insinuation that his lack of years put him on the same level as an imbecile, said shortly, "Yes, sir."

"Have you a family to support?"

"I have a mother, two sisters, and two brothers."

"All younger than you?"

"Yes, sir."

Shelley reached for his coffee, topped it generously with cognac and sipped it, meditating on Matt over the gilt rim.

"It must be very difficult for you," he remarked.

Matt said nothing. He was tired and didn't want to be pitied.

"I understand that you met my son at Marchester last summer," Mr. Shelley went on. "He told me that you fished him out of the water when he dived after that painter fellow. You saw my yacht there, the *Good Fortune*?"

"Yes, sir."

"I shall be needing deck hands for her this summer. Would you be interested in sailing with us?"

Matt looked up, his breath stopping in his throat. He didn't know if it was the cognac or the question, but his head suddenly seemed to swim.

"Yes, sir," he whispered.

"I am a busy man, and I'm often abroad," Mr. Shelley went on. "I shall not be sailing often, but I hope to get her into trim so that we can race her in the regatta. If I let you know when you're wanted, would you join her in Marchester?"

"Yes, sir."

"I should pay you well, of course. More coffee?"

"Thank you, sir." Matt felt as if he were in a dream. He watched the steam curling up from his refilled cup and through it he seemed to see the *Good Fortune* reaching out of the Marchester river, her narrow bows slicing the water, her wake hissing astern, himself at the sheets, in white trousers. . . . The vision intoxicated him. He found he was grinning like a monkey. He looked at Francis, and Francis's face was all excitement, his eyes shining.

"Father, that would be wonderful!" he said, springing up from the bunk.

Mr. Shelley smiled at him. "He might be able to teach you a thing or two, my boy, if that's what you want. I'm afraid my son is more interested in sailing than in his studies," he added to Matt. "That is why he insisted on making the trip to Amsterdam with me—and he would have nothing to do with a steam packet either. I fear for his work this coming summer when the *Good Fortune* is sailing! We both have a lot to learn, you understand. But with the right skipper and crew my ship would sweep the board."

"Oh, yes, sir. She's a beautiful boat." Matt remembered the day he had last seen her, down there on the hard with Melville and his father. He couldn't help wondering what his father would have said if this offer had been made when he was still alive. He might have let him go for the sake of the money, but he certainly wouldn't have approved.

"Were you making for home when we met you?" Mr. Shelley asked.

Matt got to his feet. "Yes, sir. I was. I must start back now, else I'll be into the Thames."

"I'll come up on deck with you and see the captain. There's the matter of remuneration for your services to be settled."

In the excitement of seeing himself on the deck of the *Good Fortune* Matt had forgotten about his present situation. He looked up with a start. In the space of a few hours money seemed to be presenting itself from every quarter. He tried to keep his face noncommittal, but quite suddenly he felt that fate had decided to shine on him, and when they emerged on deck once more into the fresh, damp air of the fine May dawn his face was alight with excitement.

Mr. Shelley went straight to the captain and addressed him in his own language. Matt stood by in silence. Shelley sounded somewhat peremptory, and the captain was annoyed, hesitant and, finally, resigned. He turned and gave an order to the mate, who hurried off.

Shelley turned to Matt. "Do you think twenty-five pounds is a fair price for your services?" he asked.

Matt swallowed. "Yes—yes, sir. Thank you."

Twenty-five pounds! His lips went dry. He stared down at the deck and it seemed to be coming and going at him. It was like the time in the cuddy when the man off the wreck had spilled the sovereigns out of the little bags. Twenty-five pounds! He did not trust himself to say any more, for his throat was tight and the cognac was mazing his head. Francis was smiling and his father was looking satisfied at the captain's obvious grief. Matt knew if it hadn't been for Mr. Shelley he would have got, perhaps, ten pounds for his help. He didn't feel sorry for the captain. He who should have known better had jeopardized his ship for money, and his subsequent sufferings were just retribution.

The mate hurried back with a bag of sovereigns which the captain counted and passed over to Matt. He shook his hand and forced a smile, and Matt said, "Thank you, sir."

"You go now?" the mate asked.

"Yes, sir."

There were handshakings all round, with the mate, Mr.

Shelley, Francis, and several of the cigar-smoking Dutchmen, who were all looking very jolly now that the schooner
was speeding into the Thames. Matt guessed they would be
jollier still when he was gone and the hampering *Fathom*
was loosed from the schooner's towrope. He went to the
stern, and the mate turned the schooner up into the wind.
Fathom slipped under the counter and Matt leaped for the
shrouds, holding his moneybag tightly in his teeth. The
next moment the tow was loosed and *Fathom* was pitching
about in the schooner's wake, dropping astern so rapidly
that, by the time her sails were hoisted, she was a toy boat
way in the distance. Francis, leaning over the rail, raised
a hand to wave and thought he saw an answering salute.

"Father, I'm glad you asked him to come on the *Good
Fortune*," he said as he straightened up. "I like him."

His father nodded. "He's a fine boy," he said. "He had
courage, all right, to take the ship across those shoals." He
smiled suddenly and put a hand on his son's shoulder.
"Well, our business trip to Amsterdam hasn't been without
its adventure, eh? And I think we might be glad of that lad
on our yacht when we take up Lord Wickford's challenge
this summer."

It was late afternoon by the time Matt got *Fathom* home.
A strong headwind off the shore had them beating stubbornly most of the morning; then a bad split in the mainsail
entailed a weary session with needle and palm.

Matt leaned wearily on the tiller as the smack tacked
through the choppy, sunlit water, feeling the bag of sovereigns in his pocket and thinking of his new job on the
Good Fortune. He had tried to explain the whole adventure of his meeting with Mr. Shelley to Aaron, but it was
like talking to a post. He showed him the bag of sovereigns

and the old man's face lit up. Matt, in his pity, opened it and put two into the scabby, wrinkled palm. Then he held up the rest and said, "For our new smack," and Aaron nodded as if he understood, tucking his two coins away with reverent care into his old leather purse.

When he got home Matt found his mother white and tired, waiting for him with his dinner.

"Whatever happened to you?" she said. "The others were home before dawn. I've been worried to death, watching for you all day. I thought you must be aground, or run down."

"No." Matt stood with a smile all over his face, the bag of sovereigns in his hand. "I was doing another job. It paid better than shrimping."

"What do you mean?" His mother looked up sharply at the clink of coins. "What have you done? Nothing your father would have been ashamed of, I hope."

She took the bag disbelievingly and looked inside.

"Twenty-three," Matt said proudly. "There were twenty-five, but I gave two to Aaron." He told her the story, brimming with excitement, so that even with the tale of adventure in her ears Mary Pullen couldn't help thinking that he looked like a boy again.

"So it was worth your worrying a bit, wasn't it, Mother? Twenty-three sovereigns for the new smack and a job through the summer—just when they're sailing, of course —but he said, 'I'd pay you well.' Those were his words. 'I'd pay you well.' And think of it, Mother, sailing on that yacht! And everyone in Marchester is fighting to get a place on her."

"Oh, Matt," said Mary Pullen, sitting down in her chair with the sovereigns in her lap. She smiled, and her lips trembled, so that she was laughing and crying at the same time. "Oh, Matt," she repeated. "Whatever would your father have said, deck hand on a yacht? I don't know what to think."

"Well, you ask George Firmin what he thinks, and old Beckett. They'd give their noses for the chance. Father was old-fashioned about yachts, but he'd have done what I did, Mother. And when I'm deck hand, it's only for a few days, when the trials are on, or they're racing. Then I fish all the rest of the time. It's a wonderful chance, Mother."

"All this money!" His mother held up the bag and looked into it again like a child. Then she closed it up and put it on the mantel-shelf and got to her feet.

"You must be tired out, Matt. You've been out two days and no food to speak of. Here, sit down! You can tell me all about it afterwards. It all sounds like a miracle to me. I don't know what to think. My head's in a whirl. Whatever will Anne and the boys say?"

She was still smiling and the tears were still trickling down her cheeks. She kept looking at the money on the mantel-shelf as she cut bread for Matt, and wondering if, perhaps, with this windfall, they would be able to buy the new smack after all. She hardly dared hope they would make their way. She had spent the last four weeks watching Matt get thinner and more silent and more weary day by day, and every day her heart had sunk a little lower and all her thoughts she had had to keep to herself, to show loyalty to Matt. She thought he could do it, but it grieved her to see him with such obligations when he was so young.

Matt finished his meal and had another look at the sovereigns in the bag, then he sat in his father's chair and stared dreamily into the fire. The *Good Fortune* was there, roaring through the flames, bow wave thundering, spray coming over in sheets . . . Matt smiled happily and, within the minute, was asleep.

The Skipper

A letter came for Matt in the middle of May. The envelope had a crest on it and the paper was thick, with an embossed address and gilt at the edges. Anne hung it up on the wall over the mantel-shelf when they had all finished marveling at it, and the perfect copperplate was there for all the world to see:

"Sir,

"Hands for the yacht, *Good Fortune,* are requested to be aboard by 10 o'clock on the morning of Wednesday, 22nd of May."

Underneath, in not such perfect copperplate, a message was scrawled: "Matt, I shall be aboard on Tuesday evening. If you can come over early, we can have a chat. You can sleep aboard Tuesday. Francis."

Although Matt had said very little about his adventure aboard the schooner, everyone seemed to know about it and Matt received congratulations from all the smacksmen. Most of them were genuinely glad about Matt's luck after what the family had gone through and George Firmin summed up the general feeling when he said, "It's the best thing that could have happened to you, Matt, and you deserve it."

"Yes, I was in the right place when that ship came past in the fog," Matt agreed. "Although at the time I didn't think so! Her bowsprit nearly went right through us."

"Our friend Beckett would have given his right arm to have been in your place, I'll bet. That's twice you've pipped him to a job."

Matt smiled uneasily. "It's not difficult to see why he dislikes me," he said quietly, "any more than it's obvious why I dislike him. Sometimes I have a feeling that—that—" He hesitated. "I mean, things get worse, or they get better. And with him, they won't get better. Sometimes I wonder what will happen."

George shrugged. "You've more friends than he has, don't worry."

"Does he want a job aboard the *Good Fortune,* too?" Matt asked.

"Aye. He's been round to Marchester to see Melville, I know for a fact. But he never said anything afterwards. There's too many Marchester men on the spot down there, seeking the same thing. I reckon you'll be the only 'foreigner' aboard."

Matt grimaced. "If the reputation of Marshfield lies in my hands, it's a poor thing for Marshfield. I don't think sailing the *Good Fortune* will be much like sailing a smack."

On the morning he was to sail round to Marchester to join the racing yacht he felt more as if he were dressing for a wedding than for work. His mother had been washing and pressing his working clothes and she and Anne between them had knitted him a new jersey. His hair had been cut, his boots polished like a hunter's saddle, his socks meticulously darned. He smelled of soap and clean washing and felt as if he were going on holiday. His mother had packed him a spare jersey and socks in a sailcloth bag, along with some bread and cheese for his lunch and some thick slices of ham.

"There now, and don't get all dirtied up sailing round, after all our trouble," she said when he was ready. "And behave yourself and don't get mixed up in any of those Marchester taverns even if the rest of them do. We'll see you when we see you, I suppose."

"I'll behave myself, Mother, don't worry."

He kissed her good-bye and Anne walked down to *Fathom* with him, hitching her skirt up out of the dew. She was envious and excited.

"I wish I was a boy," she said. "I could crew for you, better than polishing that old vicarage."

Matt thought she could, too. She was straight and strong and bold, not a prim flower of a girl like some of them.

"But it's better than going to Uncle Albert," she hurried on. "You're managing, aren't you, Matt? It will be all right? With this, I mean."

"It's all right," Matt said. He wanted to add, "Even without this," but he wasn't sure. He remembered how he had felt when *Fathom* had been at anchor in the fog.

It was a long time since he had sailed alone, and he felt very contented as the old smack butted along offshore, a good breeze on her beam, the sun picking out the myriad colors of the patches on her poor old sails.

"You'll be lucky if you get through another winter, old *Fathom*," Matt said to her, and his thoughts went to the smack race that would take place during the Marchester regatta. *Fathom,* in spite of her age, was a fast boat, and it was rumored that Mr. Shelley was putting up a special prize. If *Fathom* won it, they might have a bit more money to put towards *Reward*. He rather doubted, though, if she

could beat *Charity*; and he was sure that if she did, Beckett
would knife him some dark night soon afterwards.

It was getting on in the afternoon when *Fathom* sailed
past the *Good Fortune* off Melville's yard and dropped her
anchor just beyond on the edge of the mud. To see the big
yacht there, her paintwork gilded by the strong afternoon
sunlight, set Matt's heart racing with excitement. As he
stood on *Fathom*'s deck paying out the anchor chain he
saw someone waving to him from the yacht's stern and
recognized Francis's enthusiastic figure.

"I'll come for you in the dinghy!" The boy's voice echoed
across the water. Matt hastily stowed his sails and tidied
the deck and was ready to receive the dinghy when it came
alongside.

"I've been watching out for you," Francis said eagerly.
"I'm glad you've come early. It was a good idea of mine,
wasn't it, to ask you for tonight? Come back with me and
I'll show you over the yacht and we can have supper together. There will be no time to talk tomorrow, I'm sure."

Matt slipped down into the dinghy and sat in the stern
while Francis rowed back. He suddenly got the impression

that Francis, for all his grand position and wealth, was a lonely boy, and he felt an odd kinship with him for no reason that he could explain. It occurred to him that he was rather lonely, too, should he ever have time to think about it. Apart from his family and Aaron, only George Firmin meant anything to him at all. Perhaps this fact explained his feeling of sympathy with Francis. It was certainly through no similarity in their ways of life.

The dinghy slipped alongside the yacht's counter. Francis went aboard with the painter, and the next moment Matt was standing for the first time on the deck of the *Good Fortune,* looking round him almost with reverence. The scoured white deck was quite flush save for the hatches, and the impression it gave him was one of strength and purpose, of being stripped for her job with no concession to ladies' comforts. Matt had always rather thought that yachts such as these were for the rich to amuse themselves on, with sunshades and lounging chairs and stewards with drinks and sandwiches, but the *Good Fortune* looked as business-like as *Fathom* herself.

"Will you come below?" Francis invited.

He went forward and disappeared down a companionway and Matt followed. The companionway gave into a saloon which reminded Matt of the cabin aboard the schooner. There was no comparison to be drawn here between this yacht and *Fathom,* for any quarters farther removed from *Fathom*'s black cuddy, would have been hard to envisage. The saloon was carpeted and cushioned, lined with plush sofas and mahogany sideboards, and it had a fireplace with a mantel-shelf over it; there was even a vase of flowers standing there. Forward the door opened into a galley and forward again was the skipper's cabin, and locker space. A door aft out of the saloon led to the owner's cabin, and aft again was the guest's cabin. Francis showed Matt right through from end to end and Matt stared in wonder at the fantastic comfort and elegance: the washbasins in the cabins, the spotless sheets and pillows, the fittings in the galley with its efficient stove, and the pans hanging in rows and the wine cabinet full of bottles. It was all quite beyond anything he had imagined, in every way more civilized and more efficient. He had never dreamed that a yacht could be so palatial.

"It's magnificent," he said to Francis simply when they were back in the saloon again.

"Isn't she lovely?" Francis said. "This is the best thing my father has ever done—become interested in sailing. I only wish I knew as much about it as you did."

"But I don't know anything about *this*," Matt said. "No more than you do. An old smack—that's different. I know about that, and that is all I *do* know about. It's not much to be proud of."

"Well, as far as I can see, it's worth more than all the useless things I know," Francis said. "I spend all my time stuffing Latin and Greek and mathematics with a dried-up old tutor, preparing to go to university, where I shall spend even more time stuffing Latin and Greek and mathematics —for what? None of it makes sense to me and I hate every minute of it. It was only when we started coming down here and the yacht was building, and I saw the smacks working on the river and schooners going out and the brigs coming in and people like you doing something you were born to, that I began to wonder what I was missing. It all has a sort of—of romance about it, to me—although I don't suppose you would see it like that."

Matt didn't. "Perhaps you were born to Latin and all

that," he said, surprised at Francis's point of view. "I don't think you're missing much, not being on a smack or a brig."

"Would you rather do something else?"

Matt hesitated, remembering the scenes with Uncle Albert.

Francis said, "Your father was drowned. Didn't that put you off?"

"It doesn't mean to say I'm going to be," Matt said. "No, it didn't put me off. I suppose I wouldn't do anything else really, but that's not to say that I think it's romantic, fishing. If you came out a few times, you'd see."

"Could I? Would you take me?"

"Take you?" Matt was astonished. He had a vision of the delicate Francis Shelley shoving *Fathom*'s dinghy off the hard at Marshfield in the cold light of a February dawn, hearing the cursing and swearing that went on as the smacksmen hauled up ice-stiff sails, seeing romance in the mud and the trawl and his raw, sore hands. "Why? Is that what you want?"

"Yes. More than anything I can think of."

"You can come, all right, if your father would let you."

Matt looked at Francis curiously. His face was almost that of a girl's, with the sensitive mouth and handsome eyes, and the long auburn hair curling behind his ears, yet there was a strength, somewhere, that Matt couldn't quite define. Although he was inclined to laugh at Francis's suggestion, he knew that it took a certain amount of courage to attempt what he wanted to do.

"I don't mean just an afternoon's fishing, like a tripper," Francis added, "but the real thing. When you go back to Marshfield, perhaps I could come over and just be your crew for a day or two."

"Of course, if that's what you want."

"You mean it?" Francis persisted. "I do. If you agree, I'll ask my father to arrange it with your mother."

The conversation was interrupted by the appearance of an elderly but nimble-looking steward who had just arrived on board with some parcels of provisions. They helped him unload them down in the galley, and while he set about preparing them their supper, Matt suggested they should row across to Melville's yard and hand over the bag of sovereigns. He wanted to see them safely in Melville's hands and was afraid he might not get another opportunity. He hoped he might see *Reward,* too, on the stocks.

Melville was in his office and he jumped up when he saw the boys.

"Good afternoon, sir. Good afternoon, Mr. Pullen. What can I do for you?"

"I've brought you some more money towards the smack, sir," Matt said, holding out the bag. "Twenty pounds. It's safer with you than it would be at home."

"There's no hurry for it, lad," Melville said. "You might be needing it for something else before the smack is ready. I was very sorry to hear about your father, very sorry indeed. You knew I wouldn't be pressing you for the money, though."

"No, I know that, but I want you to have this. I may not be able to pay the rest so quickly."

"All right, I'll have it and thank you. We're getting on well with your boat, too. Ahead of ourselves we are. I should think she'd be ready for you before the winter sets in."

Matt's face lit up. "She will? That will be fine. *Fathom*'s near her end now. I don't think she'll be safe for another winter."

"Aye, we'll have the new one finished for you then. You can't go taking any risks now you're the breadwinner. D'you want to see how she's looking now you're here?"

They followed him out into the workyard, where three or four boats were in various stages of completion on the stocks. The last of the sunlight lingered on pale virgin planks; the smell of shaved wood and resin was sweet between the high brick walls. Matt's eyes went straight to the half-planked ribs of a thirty-foot vessel lying at the top of the yard. He took in the lovely lines of the grown timber, the full, strong turn of the bilge and the grace of the counter that curved up astern.

"Is that her?" he asked softly.

"Aye, that's yours."

Matt felt a thrill of anticipation go through him at the thought of owning this shining skeleton, this embryo of Melville's craft with the froth of shavings about its keel. He said nothing, for he thought the excitement a childish thing, but his eyes were shining.

"She'll suit you, eh?" said Melville.

"Oh, yes. She's—she's fine."

Melville turned to Francis with a smile. "We've room in the yard now, sir, since your father's boat was launched.

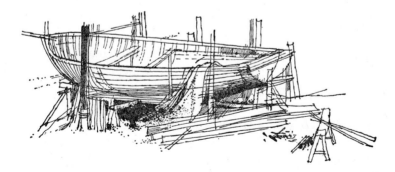

Room to move again. She fair took up our space, that one. I've never had such a monster on my stocks before."

His eyes went out to the river and rested tenderly on the aristocratic lines of the yacht. "She should go, that girl," he said. "There won't be one to touch her in the races this summer."

Francis laughed. "Lord Wickford doesn't think so. He's got a wager on with my father for the week of the regatta."

"Aye, sir, so I've heard. It's going to be an exciting year for the racing this summer, what with that and the prize your father's putting up for the smacks. Are you going to have a shot at that, Matt?"

Matt would have liked to ask what the extra prize was worth, but didn't. He shrugged. "I would if I thought my sails would stand it."

"I might find you a good mainsail for the day," Melville said. "You ought to give *Fathom* her last race. She was always a fast boat, the fastest at Marshfield."

"*Charity* could beat her."

"Oh, aye, *Charity*. Perhaps."

The two boys went back to the hard and rowed in amicable silence back to the yacht. The tide ran strongly, the water a metal gray, reflecting the first lights that were going on along the banks. Lights were shining up through the skylights when they went aboard and the steward had lit a fire in the grate. The saloon in the lamplight was warm and graceful, with the table laid for supper. A white cloth was spread with fine silver and china and wineglasses. Matt had never seen anything like it before.

"Are you waiting for your father, sir?" the steward asked Francis. "Or would you like to eat now?"

"I'm ravenous," Francis said. "My father didn't say what time he was coming, either. I think we'll eat now."

"Very well, sir."

"Here, sit down, Matt."

Matt hesitated. "I'm—I'm supposed to be a hand. Is it all right? With your father, I mean?"

Francis laughed. "Of course! He knows I've invited you down tonight. You're a hand tomorrow, but tonight you're my guest. You'll sleep here, too, I hope."

Matt sat down, obediently, wondering if Francis had really meant it when he said he would come back to Marshfield with him. He would find it a bit different there, he thought. The steward brought a meal of oysters and lamb cutlets with green peas in butter and fruit and coffee, and Francis filled the wineglasses. Matt sat taking it all in and trying to remember all the details to tell his mother. Quite suddenly, when the steward handed him a plateful of cheeses, he remembered Uncle Albert, and his joy was complete.

From Francis's conversation Matt found himself getting his first insight into this way of life that Francis apparently found so boring. To Matt it sounded as magical as sailing seemed to appear to Francis. Francis traveled abroad; he had lived in Paris and spoke fluent French; he had climbed in the Swiss mountains (Matt had never even seen a mountain); he could read Greek, and knew more theory of sail than Matt knew existed. Matt would have been awed if it had not been for Francis's genuine admiration for his own poor talents. Francis thought the ability to handle a smack far more impressive than knowing one's way about Europe, a sure hand on the tiller of more worth than a sensitive hand on the piano. If Matt thought the reasoning topsy-turvy, he hadn't the heart to disillusion Francis. Instead, warmed by his enthusiasm, Matt found himself telling the story of his life, of how they went out on the tides, the daily routine of streaming a stow net for sprats or trawling for shrimps, of sailing home, the endless work of repairing nets and sails, swabbing decks, of renewing caulking and rigging. He told Francis about the night they had sailed out to the wreck and afterwards about the day his father was drowned, although he said nothing of losing the money in the money belt. He had never talked so much in his life before, prompted by his attentive audience and the wine, and he was astonished when he realized how the evening had flown. There were footsteps on the deck above. Francis took a gold watch out of his trouser pocket and looked at it and said, "Ten o'clock. This must be my father. He is bringing the skipper aboard with him tonight, I believe."

They stood up as the footsteps clattered on the companion-way. Blinking in the sudden light, Mr. Shelley swung down into the saloon and looked around cheerfully.

"Hullo, the pair of you! I'm glad to see you again, Matt. I hope Francis has been a good host to you. Tell Henry we're here, Francis, if he hasn't heard the din already. He should be putting a meal on for us, late as we are. Where's the skipper got to? Come on down, skipper, and meet two of your new crew."

Another figure came heavily down the companionway and stepped into the saloon.

"Mr. Beckett, meet Matt Pullen, of Marshfield, and my son, Francis."

Matt froze where he stood. The hand he had half stretched out dropped back to his side as if it had been stung and he said nothing, staring at Beckett with wide angry eyes. The shock was so sudden that he couldn't have said anything even if he had wanted to. His tongue was stuck to the roof of his mouth and he could feel the color mounting in his cheeks.

There was a moment's rather surprised silence which Francis broke by stepping forward and saying something cordial to suit the occasion. Beckett then sent a malicious smile in Matt's direction and said, "Mr. Pullen and I have already met."

"Of course, Melville told me you were a Marshfield man. I'd forgotten," said Mr. Shelley. He gave Matt a rather searching look and then added, "Let's hope the two of them have left us something to eat. Come, Mr. Beckett, I'll show you your quarters while Henry gets our meal ready."

He was obviously in a very good humor. Beckett picked up his bag without a word and followed Mr. Shelley forward through the galley. Matt's eyes watched the broad back disappear and felt the shock fizzle out in his breast to a dull, angry disappointment. Beckett skipper of the *Good Fortune*! It was the last thing he had thought of. And, yet, why? he wondered miserably. For all one might think of him, Beckett was the best skipper on the coast. It hadn't seemed strange when George had suggested he had been turned down as a hand. One couldn't see Beckett as a hand, only as a skipper. Now that it had happened it seemed quite inevitable. Matt was angry with himself for having shown his feelings.

"You know Mr. Beckett then?" Francis said, looking at him closely.

"Yes, I know him. I'm sorry if I seemed rude. It was just a—a surprise to find that he was the skipper."

"I should have told you earlier," Francis said. "I should have realized you would know him, being from Marshfield. He seems a very good man. My father was pleased at getting him."

"Yes, he's a good skipper all right."

Matt felt awkward and miserable and didn't want to discuss his dismay at meeting Beckett. Nor did he want to remain in the saloon when Beckett came back. He stood hesitantly, fidgeting with the edge of the tablecloth and Francis said, "Shall we go to bed, then? They'll want to talk, I suppose."

Matt nodded, with a great feeling of relief.

Francis waited until the two men came back, to excuse them both.

"Very well, you'll want to be feeling fit in the morning," Mr. Shelley said. "Mr. Beckett will be finding plenty for you to do, I'm sure."

He laughed cheerfully.

"Good night, sir. Good night, Mr. Beckett," Francis said. Beckett was standing with his back to the fire, in his hand the glass of port that Mr. Shelley had just poured him.

"Good night, sir," he said to Francis. "Good night, Mr. Pullen."

Across the saloon Matt felt Beckett's shrewd black eyes resting on him. Beckett was a big man of about forty, with powerful broad shoulders like a bull, and never had he seemed to Matt quite so menacing as he stood there, his eyes mocking him across the bright saloon. In that glance Matt could read Beckett's triumph. It was the first time he had been face to face with the man he thought of as his enemy, and he knew his fear and mistrust had not been ill founded. He felt suddenly that the *Good Fortune* was a trap, and the price he was paying to come aboard her was too high: Tomorrow he would be at Beckett's mercy, taking orders from the man he most despised and hated. But it was too late to back out. He muttered a good night and followed Francis through the main cabin to the neat little guest cabin beyond, where the steward had put hot water out for them and turned back the sheets. They washed and got into the bunks and Francis turned out the lamp. Matt lay on his back staring up into the darkness, the strange and wonderful happiness of this evening extinguished by the vision of Beckett's arrogant face across the saloon.

After a while Francis said quietly, "Why wouldn't you shake hands with Mr. Beckett?"

Matt was glad that in the darkness Francis could no longer see his face nor read his thoughts. He thought for a few moments and said, "Don't ask me about Beckett. It's a private thing, and I cannot tell you."

Francis said meekly, "I'm sorry."

"It's nothing that matters," Matt lied. "I'm sorry if I offended your father."

In the darkness Matt soon heard the slow regular breathing that told him Francis was asleep. But he lay awake a long time, listening to the distant murmur of voices from the saloon and thinking of Beckett.

Beckett's Threat

The following morning the *Good Fortune* slipped away early on the tide, cheered on her way by ragged shouts from the watermen. With the wind on her beam she was out to sea within half an hour and as the low coast fell away astern she lay over and the water came hissing over her decks, leaping under her slicing bows, hurrying away astern in a mass of foam. The first day with the sun shining, the wind strong, and the sea breaking green and white right out to the horizon, was a tangled impression to Matt of excitement and fear, of the most intoxicating pleasure and exhilaration and pride, and of weariness and a deep satisfaction. In spite of Beckett, there were moments during that week which Matt knew he would never forget.

Mr. Shelley was one of the old-fashioned school who believed in leaving his yacht's performance in the hands of the professionals. Although he and his friends were usually in the cockpit with Beckett, they seldom lent a hand to a sheet, and even Francis had to keep out of the way, for Beckett's orders were to sail the yacht to her limit, and he couldn't be bothered with greenhorns (especially greenhorns he couldn't shout at). With the wager at stake Shelley

136

was taking his sailing seriously. He was no sentimentalist
and he intended to win. This suited Beckett. Matt often
thought rather bitterly that Mr. Shelley had chosen his
skipper well, for Beckett was no sentimentalist either; he
certainly did not spare his crew. And least of all did he
spare Matt. All the unpleasant jobs came Matt's way, as
Matt had known they would the moment he had discovered who his skipper was; and when the Shelleys were
out of the way he came in for plenty of abuse. Knowing
this goading was the price he must pay for sailing on the
Good Fortune, Matt treated Beckett with wary contempt
and took good care not to be found wanting. Sometimes the
effort had him muttering with vexation at the injustice of
it all, but the stubbornness with which he had once impressed his Uncle Albert stood him in good stead.

When the yacht came back to her anchor after her day's
trials the hands dispersed to their various homes and Matt
went to sleep aboard *Fathom*. Francis at first wanted him to
sleep on the yacht as he had before, but Matt refused, not
wanting to be in any way a preferred employee, especially
with Beckett at hand to remark upon his ripening friendship with Francis. Generally Matt would go ashore and buy
some bread and cheese at the nearest shop (carefully avoiding his uncle's), then he would eat in Melville's yard and
inspect his beloved *Reward,* and sometimes later Francis
would join him and they would stroll among the quays
and look at the various craft loading and unloading. During
these excursions while Francis eagerly asked him for his
technical opinions about what was going on on the river,
Matt found he had time for quite a few questions himself.
They were an assorted lot, too, and as the days went past he
learned how to read charts and how to tell a real diamond
from a fake; he learned how Nelson won the battle of

Trafalgar by superior seamanship, what to do if he fell down a crevasse, how to ask for a glass of beer in French, and the correct way to address the Queen. He considered his own rough homilies on the ways of sailing craft amply repaid.

One evening when Matt had gone ashore Francis rowed after him and caught him up as he was going up through Melville's yard.

"Here, let me come and eat with you," he said. "The yacht's crowded tonight and I prefer your company to theirs any day. Are you going to get some cheese or something? We could eat it down on the wharf. A tea clipper came in this morning. Did you see her? Let's find her. She looked magnificent."

Matt was perfectly happy to stroll towards the town with Francis. It was a warm, fair evening and he was pleasantly tired, his face burning from the day at sea, his thoughts lingering happily on this week of opportunity. The *Good Fortune* had proved his good fortune too, and even Beckett's presence had not taken away the new and exhilarating pleasure of sailing a yacht such as Mr. Shelley's. A whole new future seemed to be opening up to him. (Matt conveniently forgot at such moments that in two days' time he would be back shrimping on old *Fathom*.)

"Here," Francis said suddenly, breaking in on his thoughts and taking him by the arm, "this is where Henry gets our provisions. It's a good shop for cheese. Let me buy you something tonight."

And before Matt could protest he found himself hustled up the steps of Uncle Albert's shop and propelled through the door. The bell tinkled and in his nostrils again was the smell of cheese and spice, of tea and carbolic, the strange mixture of fragrance and odor whose sum total spelled to him only one thing: Uncle Albert. Matt stood beside Francis, wishing himself anywhere but where he was, sickened by the cool, scented atmosphere which had threatened him so vitally a few weeks earlier. But he had reckoned without the magical effect his companion would have on his uncle, and afterwards he had to admit that the visit was worthwhile just to see the various expressions that chased each other across his uncle's face when he saw the two of them together. He bowed and smiled in his oiliest manner when he saw Francis, and then gasped at the sight of Matt. A frantic curiosity shone in his beady eyes, and he looked from one to the other stupidly, his mouth opening and shutting like a fish's.

"I—I—what can I do for you, sir?" he stammered. His eyes then pierced Matt viciously.

"What shall we have, Matt?" Francis asked cheerfully. "I fancy a Camembert. What do you say? We can buy one of those brown loaves at the baker's and some fruit down on the wharf. Would that suit you?"

"Fine." Matt nodded.

"A Camembert then, and make it a good one," Francis said to Uncle Albert.

"Certainly, sir."

Uncle Albert sent a minion scurrying for boxes of Camembert which he then opened for Francis to examine, while Matt stood back and gazed tactfully into the recess of the shop. When Francis was satisfied and the cheese was being wrapped Uncle Albert sent Matt another venomous look, and unable to contain his curiosity any longer, said, "What brings you to Marchester, Matt?"

"I'm working for Mr. Shelley, Uncle," Matt said steadily, and with considerable inner satisfaction. His uncle's nostrils quivered, but he said nothing. He handed Francis his

change with another bow and a scrape and chivvied his
wretched boy to open the door for them. As Matt went out
he looked at the boy, who could so nearly have been himself, and gave him a smile that the lad puzzled over for
days. When they were outside, Francis said to Matt, "Did
you call that oaf uncle?"

"Yes. He is my uncle," Matt said.

Francis gasped and went red. "Whatever did I say? I'm
so sorry! I had no idea he was really your uncle! I do
apologize—"

Matt grinned. "Don't worry. You can't hate him more
than I do."

"But I shouldn't have said that. I don't know what I was
thinking of. I've nothing against him—it's just that he's so
—so obsequious."

"He's an unpleasant character," Matt agreed equably.
"It's strange," he added, after they had bought a loaf of
crusty new bread at the adjoining bakery, "but there are
only two people in the whole world that I have reason to—
to dislike, and you have met them both."

"Mr. Beckett and that grocer?"

"Yes. I don't want you to think that I go round hating
everybody."

"You mean that both those men have done you a wrong?
It's more than just disliking their characters?"

"Yes," Matt said briefly. He knew that Francis was hoping
he would say more, but he didn't; he was sorry the subject
of his aversion to Beckett had cropped up again, but he
wanted Francis to know that he had his reasons for his
strange behavior.

"My uncle hasn't actually done me a wrong," he felt
forced to add, "but he and I don't see eye to eye. That's all
there is to it. He wanted me to work in his shop when my

father was drowned, and I refused. He wanted to 'thrash sense into me.'" He was able to smile at the recollection now and it gave him an unaccustomed satisfaction. Life this last week had really been quite different from anything that had happened to him before.

Presently they were down on the wharf, where the tea clipper was already discharging her cargo and, seated on some convenient bales, they divided up the bread and cheese with a sheath knife and ate their supper, their eyes resting on the rakish masts of the lovely ship before them. Francis, selecting an apple from the bag of fruit, said, almost casually, "Last night I asked my father whether I could go fishing with you."

"What did he say?" Matt asked.

"He said I could," Francis said. "I think he's going to arrange it with your mother. Do you mind?"

"Mind? Why ever should I?"

"Well, I thought afterwards that I didn't give you much opportunity to refuse. I shall probably get in your way frightfully."

"You'll be good company. Old Aaron gets a bit depressing day after day, just mumbling to himself."

"I want to work, though, not just be company."

"Oh, yes." Matt grinned. "I'll make you work all right."

"Like Mr. Beckett."

"I'll out-Beckett Beckett." Matt smiled again as another thought struck him. "He'll be a bit surprised when he sees you on *Fathom*."

"Why? Will he be there too?"

"He'll be fishing in the fleet unless he's staying aboard the *Good Fortune*."

"No. He's being paid off like everyone else until the next trials. You mean he fishes with you?"

"Yes. There are about twenty boats at Marshfield and we work together most of the time."

Francis looked surprised. Matt wondered what he was expecting if he came out fishing. He seemed to think that the smacks were romantic. Matt couldn't see it himself. But for all the disparity between them, he liked Francis.

When it grew dark they walked back along the quays to Melville's yard. As they passed the lovely ribs of *Reward* gleaming in the wood-scented dusk, Matt remembered their conversation with Melville earlier in the week and asked Francis the question that had been rankling in his mind ever since.

"Is it true that your father is putting up a special prize for the smack race in the regatta?"

"Yes. He's making it twenty-five pounds," Francis replied.

"Twenty-five pounds!"

Matt stopped in his tracks. Twenty-five pounds! If he entered and won, then *Reward* would be almost paid for! *If* he won it. His mind roved over the possibilities. Twenty-five pounds was worth trying for, whatever the odds. Up till now he hadn't seriously considered entering *Fathom* with her poor ragged sails.

"Are you going in for it?" Francis asked.

"Twenty-five pounds is a lot of money," Matt said cautiously.

Francis laughed. "Yes, it's going to be an expensive regatta for my father, especially if he loses his wager with Lord Wickford."

"Why, what is the wager worth?" Matt asked. "Everyone is talking about it. What's this Lord Wickford's yacht like?"

"*Juno*? She's supposed to be the fastest thing sailing. Lord Wickford thinks so, anyway. He's bringing her round from

Cowes especially for this challenge, and they've wagered a thousand pounds each on their boat's winning."

"A thousand pounds!" Matt's voice was incredulous. "You meant if we don't win, your father is going to lose a thousand pounds?"

"Yes, and he won't be the only one," Francis said. "All his friends have got a bet on her, too."

Matt stopped in his tracks, his head spinning. And he had just been thinking that twenty-five pounds was a lot of money! What a bumpkin he was, to think that Shelley was racing for a sovereign or two and the feel of the wind on his face! Matt felt a great disillusionment settle on him.

"I never realized . . ." he faltered.

He had a lot to think about as he went back to the dark cuddy on *Fathom* and curled up on the bunk. The next day was the last day of the trials and he felt he had learned a lot during the week, and not only about being a deck hand. There were to be two more weeks of trials before the regatta at the end of July, by which time Matt knew that the six of them, under Beckett, would be a skilled and experienced crew. But now he understood why their training was to be so thorough. What a week, he thought, as he drowsed off to the familiar sound of tapping halyards and grating chain . . . there would be even less "romance" in fishing than usual when this was over, even if he was destined to have Mr. Shelley's son and heir as crew.

The next day the *Good Fortune* was sailed hard and her crew chivvied as the stop watches clicked inexorably in the hands of Mr. Shelley and his friends. Matt came in for even more rating than usual and was conscious of Beckett's black eyes boring into him, as if he knew that this was the last day he had him where he wanted him and he was making the most of it. Out into deep water the *Good Fortune* sailed, thundering through a cloud of spray to this fine summer wind. And Matt, braced by the jib sheet and seeing the horizon through a cloud of iridescent mist, thought his job worth all the rancor he suffered from Beckett.

The next trials were to be in a month's time. When the hands were paid off they were told the date they would be required. Matt memorized it carefully as he tucked away his money. Melville had been right when he said Mr. Shelley was a generous man: Matt felt he had been paid for the best holiday of his life. By comparison the prospect of fishing on the morning's tide did nothing to inspire him with enthusiasm. It was only the thought of having Francis for company some time during the week that gave him encouragement.

"Father wants to speak to you about my going fishing," Francis said after the rest of the hands had disappeared.

"Yes, that's right, Matt," Mr. Shelley agreed. "This boy of mine has been badgering me for weeks now to let him try his hand at fishing with you. He told me you'd agreed to it, so I sent Henry to see your mother, and I'm glad to say she's willing to take him on."

Henry had reported to his employer that Matt's home was spotless, his mother a respectable and intelligent woman, and the family meticulously cared for. If Mr. Shelley wasn't quite as keen on Francis's idea as the boy himself, he was careful not to let his apprehension show. Having taken the precaution of reserving a room for the trusted Henry at the local inn for the period of Francis's stay in order that he might keep a careful, if necessarily distant, eye on him, he felt he had guarded against exposing his son to any possible dangers. To guard him from hardship was another matter, but as Francis was perversely determined to seek it, his father was hoping that a short unadulterated spell of living and working as a smacksman would cure him once and for all of his ridiculous notions.

"Well, I'm giving him my blessing and I'm hereby absolving you from all responsibility if he falls overboard and drowns himself, so you'll have nothing on your conscience." Mr. Shelley's eyes were amused as he faced the two boys. "It might do him some good," he added in a more thoughtful vein, "to see what real work is like. I'm expecting him to be treated as one of the family. No privileges."

"Yes, sir."

"That's settled, then. I understand he wants to sail back with you when you go. When will you be leaving?"

"I shall sail on this tide. We shall be home by midnight."

"Get your things together then, boy," Shelley said abruptly to Francis. "Henry will row you both across to the smack."

Beckett had disappeared. Whether he knew of this arrangement or not Matt never knew, but he was glad that when he pulled up *Fathom*'s anchor and gave Francis his first order at the helm no one was there to witness this strange reversal of their stations. Francis looked very clean and delicate aboard the tarred old smack and Matt was still rather uncertain about what he expected to learn, but once *Fathom* was underway and sailing down past the straggling outbuildings of Marchester's waterfront Matt was suddenly aware of that pleasant sense of kinship again. *Fathom* might be a poor thing compared to the yacht, but she was at this moment their own to do as they pleased with, the two of them together, and it gave Matt an unexpected sense of freedom to be in charge of her again. And if there was to be a companion with him aboard his smack, there was no one he would rather have than Francis.

They were both tired after their day on the *Good Fortune*

and they did not speak much as *Fathom* beat her way out to sea. The moon was pantomime bright, unreal, the sea a sentimental flood of silver. It made Francis ache to look at it, and its beauty, together with the glow of satisfaction he felt at the thought of starting on what he considered the first real adventure of his life, put him into an almost trancelike state of joy. Nothing he had experienced on the *Good Fortune* came anywhere near to the satisfaction he felt in the spread of *Fathom*'s workaday decks beneath his feet, the smell of her cuddy, the tangle of nets stowed on her foredeck. Matt was content, but he would have been better pleased with a fair tide all the way. He had no idea of the way Francis thought.

They got into the Marshfield creek in the small hours, poling the last leg against the ebb. The creek, bare, moon-washed, with smacks heeled over on the mud, silent and forlorn, pleased Matt with its familiarity. He threw out *Fathom*'s anchor and roughly stowed her sails, and together they dragged the dinghy up the mud and onto the hard, digging in her kedge. Francis looked back down the narrow, glinting channel of water and stood listening for a moment to the sucking of the mud in the outfalls. Then he went up on the sea wall and looked across the saltings out to sea, and back up the hill to the dark hummock of the village and the elm trees round the church. Matt stood beside him for a minute.

"That's *Charity,* Beckett's smack," he said, pointing out the cutter off the hard. He knew that she had been worked by Beckett's brothers while Beckett had been skippering the *Good Fortune,* not lying idle like *Fathom.*

They walked up the hill to the cottage. It was locked up and Matt had to throw pebbles at his mother's window before she came down to let them in. In the candlelight her face was pleased and excited to have him back, then slightly doubtful at the sight of Francis.

"Mother, this is Francis. He's going to help me on *Fathom* for a few days."

Mary Pullen gave Francis an uncertain nod. "Yes. I was expecting you. I'm pleased to have you here," she said. "I hope you'll be comfortable. We're a bit cramped with six of us in this little place, but I'm sure you're welcome."

"Thank you very much," Francis said. He looked a little embarrassed and spoke shyly.

"He'll sleep with me, Mother," Matt said. "We'd sleep anywhere tonight, so don't put yourself out."

"There's some soup on the fire. I'll put you out a bowlful each. You'll feel like it if you've sailed round from Marchester tonight."

They had the soup and then went up to bed. Francis lay beside Matt, looking at the sloping roof above his head and the white light that streamed in through the small window set like an eye in the thatch. Marchester and the *Good Fortune* were not far away, yet it seemed to Francis that they were half a world away as he lay listening to the sound of Matt's breathing beside him.

Francis learned what it was like to be a smacksman. He didn't think he could ever learn to *be* a smacksman, for the subject seemed more complex to him than any of the arts required of him by his tutor, but he learned the feel of it, and the weariness and the smell of it, and his hands blistered, his skin peeled in the bright wind, and his body discovered for the first time in its life the meaning of physical effort. It was the revelation he had expected it to be. He was not disappointed.

If the other smacksmen knew who Francis was, or were amused by Matt's green crew, they made no sign. Francis was accepted as a friend of Matt's, and he made it clear from the beginning that he was prepared to work hard. After the first uncertainty, Matt soon found that he was giving him orders without a qualm. Another week, he thought, and he'd be swearing at him like a real skipper. The day's work, apart from being physically lighter with the help of a third hand, seemed to Matt far easier merely by the distraction of Francis's company, and he realized how much he had been missing articulate companionship during the last month, with only Aaron aboard. In fact, the week was something like an extension of his "holiday" in Marchester. The weather was fair and there were times when they were able to sprawl on the deck in the sun and talk and laugh. Matt had no other thoughts now than for his immediate future. There was this new friendship with Francis which, if only a fleeting thing (for Matt could see no future in it), gave him a pleasure he had never known before; there was the yacht-racing to come and, when the summer was over, the promise of his new smack, his sound, round-bellied *Reward* who would take him into the winter estuary without a quiver in her garboards. Since the nightmare of his father's death and the threat of entering Uncle Albert's establishment, the summer now seemed full of promise and opportunity.

The only figure who had the power to shake his confidence was Beckett. One night as *Fathom* was reaching home up the creek, Beckett put *Charity* about to go into the last dog's leg of the channel in such a way that Matt had to put his helm over to miss him. It was a deliberate action which put *Fathom* on the mud. The tide was making and she soon came free, but Matt was so angry that his hands were shaking on the helm as they followed *Charity* home. He put *Fathom* aground on the edge of the channel, threw out his anchor, and jumped off into the mud before Francis could guess what he intended to do. Beckett was standing on the hard, watching him, waiting for him, Matt realized afterwards.

"You filthy swine!" Matt shouted. "Who do you think you are? If I'd had a sound boat, I'd have rammed you in two pieces! You won't play tricks on me when I've got my new smack, you see! *Charity* can look out for herself then."

"Is Melville taking pity on you then?" Beckett said calmly, staring him full in the face with his mocking black eyes.

Matt stopped short. His anger gave way to a cool quiet venom as he stood looking up into Beckett's scornful face.

"Melville won't need to take pity on me," he said softly. "The new smack is half paid for already. No one will deny it me now, not even a man who will steal money off a dead man."

Beckett's eyes shifted with sudden alarm, and an ugly crimson flush stained his neck.

"You had better take care of your tongue, Matt Pullen," he said viciously, "for if you don't, there will be no skipper to sail this new smack when she is finished."

He reached out an arm and caught Matt by the folds of his jersey round the neck, pulling him close. The grip of his one hand was as strong as a vise, and Matt was powerless, caught close against that evil face, feeling the breath on his cheek that came rapidly between Beckett's broken yellow teeth. Matt did not struggle, aware for all his brave anger a moment ago that he was helpless against Beckett.

"You watch your step, Matt," Beckett said. "I'm warning you."

The voice was low, almost a whisper, but the threat was as clear as a flash of lightning. But the moment the words were out Matt saw a sudden change of expression come over

Beckett's face, and behind him from the water he heard a quick splash of footsteps.

"Mr. Beckett, take your hands off Matt!"

Francis's voice cut through the dusk, sounding in that dramatic moment exactly like his father's. Matt stumbled back as Beckett's hand relaxed. Beckett stood there on the hard, his eyes blazing with anger, but he said nothing to Francis. He stared at him as if he could have broken him

in two pieces along with Matt, but his lips were shut tight. And in an instant he had turned on his heel and marched swiftly away up the hard.

Matt looked at Francis with relief, but no great sense of victory. Francis was his protector now, because he was Mr. Shelley's son, but Francis would be gone in two days' time, and Beckett's threat would stay in Matt's mind long after that. Francis was looking angry and astonished.

"Whatever came over him?" he said.

"Nothing came over him," Matt said, pulling down his jersey. "That's Beckett."

"But he can't treat you like that. He was in the wrong, not you."

"Yes, that's what I told him, but it didn't help much, did it?" Matt said bitterly.

"He's a strange man, that Beckett," Francis said doubtfully. "My father has never seen him behave that way."

"Your father never will," said Matt. "If Beckett sails *Good Fortune* to please him, it's no concern of his what Beckett's about in his own time."

They stood together on the hard, watching the water creeping up over the mud and stones, smelling the strong, sour smell of the mud and the salt and the seaweed. Matt, looking down the widening channel of water to the sails that were slipping up towards them on the tide, had a sense of foreboding. Beckett seemed to be involved in everything important, good and bad, that had ever happened to him, as if in some way the two of them were bound together by some ironic quirk of fate. Where would it lead to, this sparking of flints every time their paths crossed? Matt knew he had no defense, not after Francis had gone back.

Together they went back down the mud to unload their catch.

Henry was not averse to spending a week at the Plough and Sail on Mr. Shelley's orders. It was virtually a holiday, for he did not think Francis would either want or need his counsel, although he sympathized with his master's doubts. Francis was Peregrine Shelley's only son and was being carefully schooled to succeed to a well-known and valuable business. He certainly wasn't accustomed to hard work in the physical sense, but Henry couldn't see that it would do him any harm. Rather the opposite. The poor lad got little enough rest from his books as it was. In fact, Henry considered that Mr. Shelley could thank his lucky stars that his son's waywardness was taking such a harmless course. A fanatical interest in working sail was a better relaxation from his studies than wine, women, and song. And if that was the way he felt, he could certainly have no better guide than Matt Pullen. In Henry's opinion Matt was a brave and honest lad. The landlord of the Plough and Sail substantiated this.

"Aye, a good boy. His mother's a lucky woman."

Having met Matt's mother, Henry thought that the woman was not so much lucky as responsible for Matt's being what he was, but he agreed mildly with the landlord.

"It was sad, the father going like that," he remarked, to draw the landlord out. They were alone in the comfortable saloon. The landlord was polishing his glasses and Henry, having had the leisure to reflect on his two Marshfield acquaintances, Matt and Beckett, was interested in knowing a little more. His mild curiosity warmed the old gossip of a landlord.

"Aye, it was sad. Not only the father, but the money as well."

"The money?" Henry prompted.

He was rewarded by learning the story of the *Seaflower*

money, of how Beckett had missed it by his callous disregard of human life, and how the Pullen family in their
turn had lost it with Tom Pullen's death.

"There's always been a deal of tongue-wagging as to
where it went to," the landlord went on. "They never found
it trawling, and there's many will swear Tom Pullen never
loosed that buckle while there was breath in his body. Well,
who's to know? There's another theory though, not that
many will give tongue to it."

He waited for Henry to prompt him, which he did with
a mere raising of one eyebrow.

"There's proof Beckett took his smack out that night. He
knew what Tom Pullen had in his belt all right—it was no
secret. He knew where the body went down, too. It's not so
hard to find a body when you've got good reason to."

Henry had unearthed more by his prompting than he ever
dreamed existed. Although nothing more than polite interest showed on his face, he was well satisfied with his haul.
It explained a good deal to him, not least the odd first meeting of Matt and Beckett on board the *Good Fortune* which
he had both overheard and overlooked through the saloon
door. It also proved something that he had felt in his bones
all along: Beckett, for all that he was a first-class skipper,
was not a man to be trusted.

He shook his head at the landlord's suspicions to show
his sympathy and suggested, "Beckett's up to tricks of that
sort, then?"

"There's no sort of trick Beckett isn't up to," the landlord
said bluntly. "He's a rogue, and a clever one, for no one has
caught him yet."

With his interest in Beckett quickened by the landlord's
tale, Henry found himself watching the man closely when
he visited the inn. If Beckett was surprised to find Henry

on his home ground, he did not show it, nor did he go out of his way to be friendly. He kept himself very much to himself, chatting only with his brothers. It was plain that he was far from popular with the rest of the smacksmen, but he was treated with a deference that impressed Henry. His shrewdness and his wealth had made him a powerful figure in the village. It did not take Henry long to discover that in only five years Beckett had come to own the largest smack, with a second one building, a row of cottages, a horse and cart, and several acres of land. "On shrimping!" The landlord spat contemptuously. Henry, raising his glass, noted Beckett's broad shoulders across the saloon, the cunning eyes and the easy, dangerous grace of his big body. Mr. Shelley's manservant, thoughtful and unobtrusive in his corner, did not envy young Matt Pullen his enemy.

The Eve of the Regatta

Matt ran *Fathom* onto the mud off Melville's yard, put out his anchor, and went ashore. Up through the wood shavings and stacks of oak and pitch pine he found his smack, planked now and her decks half finished, as sweet and as shapely as he had always dreamed of her. A deep satisfaction seized him as he sniffed the pale new wood. It smelled not yet of tar and fish and bilge water, but of resin and sunshine and forests. "My old boat," he said softly, and he put his hand up and stroked the lovely curve of her hull. Across the water the *Good Fortune* rested like a migrant bird. Matt could sense anticipation in the air; the atmosphere of the old sailing town *en fête* for the regatta was infectious. Visiting boats lay at all angles on the mud, and rowing skiffs skulled about like water beetles. There were flags flying off the Customs House; tonight the taverns would be full. The streets would be full of light and laughter, and there would be brawls and confusion, singing and fighting.

He turned and went across the yard to the sheds and lofts to find Melville. The old man was sorting through papers in his office, and smiled when he saw Matt.

"Ah, you are here for the excitement, then. I want to see that yacht of ours beat the foreigner, my lad. The whole town's got its money on her."

"Aye, I hope she does. We can't have her beaten. We'd never hold up our heads again."

"That's right. There's a lot at stake. And how about the smacks? Are you racing your old *Fathom*?"

"I will if you've got a mainsail to lend me," Matt said. "Her sails are nearly done. They won't stand a beating."

"Aye, I'll lend you sails. I said I would, although it's not a thing I would do for everyone. You come up tomorrow and I'll have them out for you. Bend them on in the evening and she'll be all ready for the racing Wednesday."

"Thank you, sir!"

"You win, lad. You deserve some luck."

Matt smiled. If he won, the money would be Melville's; he wasn't sure if that's what Melville meant when he exhorted him to win. The old man had a twinkle in his eye.

Matt went outside again to head for the quays, but as he stepped out of the yard gate a horse cab drew up and Francis got down, along with the steward Henry and a whole lot of luggage. Francis looked very different from when Matt had last seen him, dressed in a fashionable suit with a cravat and immaculately pressed trousers. Matt remembered him on the Marshfield hard all covered in mud and laden with shrimp baskets, and he was surprised again at their incongruous friendship. Whenever he thought of it, it was with a sense of incredulity.

"Matt!" Francis cried, his face lighting up. "How good to see you again! Have you seen *Juno* yet? Here, wait for me, will you? I'll go aboard and change and we'll go out and see the sights while we've got the chance. My father will be down later."

Matt helped Henry load stores while Francis changed, and an hour later they were strolling together towards the quays. Since they had last said good-bye in Marshfield, Matt had spent two more separate weeks of trials on the *Good Fortune,* but Francis had been in Paris with his tutor and had missed them.

"I was sorry," he said. "I would far rather have been on board than studying over there."

He meant it, too, Matt knew. He made Paris sound as commonplace as Marshfield saltings.

"How was Beckett?" he asked, frowning. "I said nothing to my father, as you made me promise, but I've thought a lot about it since."

"He was all right," Matt said briefly. No one knew but the other hands the jobs Beckett had found Matt when Mr. Shelley was away: the scrubbing and polishing, the fetching and carrying, scraping the dinghy, loading water, running messages; three times as much work as any of the other hands. There were curses and cuffs which Matt had found hard to bear and nights when he had lain in *Fathom*'s cuddy close to tears at his humiliation. But since it was all part of the price he had to pay for working on the yacht, he accepted it. Francis was the last person who was likely to hear of Matt's persecution.

"I enjoyed that week with you, Matt," Francis said suddenly. "I thought about it often when I was in Paris. I expect you will think I'm talking nonsense, but it was one of the best weeks of my life."

Matt smiled. He didn't know what to say. He couldn't pretend to understand Francis, only perhaps to realize that the conventions of the rich could be as narrow and restricting to a boy as the continual grind of work could sometimes be wearisome to a smacksman like himself.

"I reckon you made a better fisherman than I'd ever make a scholar," he said.

"If I could do a fraction of what you can do with a boat, I'd be happy," Francis said. "You know, if you'd have me again, I'd like to come and fish with you in the winter."

"It's—it's different then. I'd have the new smack, though." But Matt never for a moment dreamed that Francis would remember this wish when the sailing season was over.

"Are you entering *Fathom* for the smack race?"

Matt's face lit up. "Yes. Melville is lending me sails. He's going to have them out for me tomorrow."

"Who is crewing for you?" Francis asked. "Aaron?"

"No, he'd be no good for racing. But there are always boys who will crew. I'll find someone."

Francis hesitated, then said, "Would you take me?"

"You?" The possibility had never crossed Matt's mind. He looked up in surprise. "Yes, why not? I'd never thought of you wanting to come. I might want a third, too, though. Perhaps one of George's brothers . . ."

They walked down the riverbank to look at *Juno,* moored just downstream from *Good Fortune*. Matt's nerves quivered as he looked at the silhouette on the water, the mast slender against the sun that was going down now in a sky of lurid ribbons over the saltings. The river ran quietly, gold and crimson, under the narrow bows. She was tranquil enough now, the yacht at anchor, the shadow of her mast touching the bank, but Matt was remembering the thunder of the creaming mass of water under the *Good Fortune*'s lee rail, the rainbow clouds of spray about her bows, and the fierce power of the sails with the wind in them. They belied it all, the excitement and the speed and the thrill, the slender hulls of the rival yachts lipping at the tide like a pair of stabled horses, docile on their tethers. The two boys looked at them and discussed their merits and chances, as the whole of Marchester was then doing, then walked back into the dusking, gaslit town, where already the taverns were noisy and the eating places full of "foreigners."

The next day the *Good Fortune*'s crew reported for duty early, and the day was spent cleaning, scouring, polishing, checking warps and blocks and halyards, and making sure that not a thing was out of place. The weather was mild and sunny, the wind light from the west, and all day long forecasts were being made for the next morning; the same wind but a little more of it was what they wanted. The crew of the *Good Fortune* was in good spirits and the work went well. Excitement was running high. Personal pride saw to it that no tasks were skimped. The race was due to start at ten the next morning at the mouth of the river, and the crew was dismissed early, ostensibly so that they could get a good night's sleep, but Matt guessed that most of them would find an excuse to join in the evening's revelry up in the town. For himself, he intended to devote the evening to *Fathom*. She might not come up as bright as the *Good Fortune*, but she could at least be clean and tidy for her race.

He got a lift across to *Fathom*, collected his dinghy, and rowed ashore to fetch his sails. Mr. Shelley had issued all his crew with resplendent white jerseys with *Good Fortune* worked across the chest, and Matt felt rather pleased with himself as he went up through the yard to the lofts. Melville chaffed him, bundling up a great red mainsail that warmed Matt's heart, not quite new but as strong and sound as *Charity*'s.

"Put this in your arms, my lad, and your white jersey will be tanned for the racing. Here, I've a topsail you can have, too, if you're wanting one, and I don't suppose your jib is up to much, eh? Might as well have the lot while you're here. I'm as keen for you to win this race as you are yourself, you know!"

And he roared with laughter, with big winks at his foreman, while Matt stripped off the white jersey and picked up the great bundle of the mainsail.

"Here, I'll help you with that," the foreman said, and between them they carried it out to the rowing boat. With the white jersey folded reverently on the thwart, Matt rowed his precious cargo of sails back to *Fathom* and heaved them onto the deck. Then he set about the task of bending them on. As he worked he thought he saw Beckett watching him from the stern of the *Good Fortune* and he was pleased at the idea of disturbing Beckett. For Beckett would know what the new sails meant, and he wasn't likely to be pleased at *Fathom*'s improvement.

"We'll give *Charity* something to think about tomorrow," Matt said to himself. He did not dare to think that he might win tomorrow. Better to keep thoughts of winning for the *Good Fortune*.

The sun went down in a crimson haze across the river. Matt saw Beckett leave for the hard, and later Mr. Shelley, Francis and some guests were rowed ashore by Henry to attend a dinner in town. The river was silent, lights glancing here and there off the ebbing tide. The wind had died, the stars were sharp over the sail lofts like pricks in a dark curtain. Matt put on his white jersey again and leaned on his tiller, listening to the ebb under the rudder. He felt tired and excited, full of apprehension for the morning, and buoyed up at the same time with a happiness he had never known before. Here from his tiller, it seemed to him at that moment, he could almost put his hand on everything tangible that composed his happiness: his own *Fathom* with her borrowed sails, *Reward* up in Melville's yard, the *Good*

Fortune . . . It was a brief, strange moment of utter contentment—but only a moment, for almost at once a figure appeared on the *Good Fortune*'s counter and a hail across the water startled Matt out of his dream.

"Ahoy, *Fathom*! Matt, are you there?"

Matt recognized Henry's voice, and hailed him back. Henry shouted for him to come over and Matt, with a sigh of resignation, cast off in his dinghy and rowed over. Henry passed him down a purse of money with instructions to go up to a tavern called The Barge and fetch down some ale for the morning.

"If there's any celebrating to be done, I doubt if I'll have enough for the hands," Henry said. "The landlord there knows me. He's promised me some brandy, too—he said he'd send it down to the yacht tonight, but I've seen no sign of it yet, so ask him if he's forgotten. And don't loiter, lad. It'll be busy up there."

Matt tucked the money away inside his belt and rowed across to Melville's yard. He wasn't sorry for an excuse to go ashore, and he whistled as he hurried along the quays. The Barge was at the top of the long hill leading up from the water to the market square. As he passed the swirling, bawling Black Horse, the smoke-hazy Ferryboat, the Dog and Duck resounding with harmonica music and song, and the crowded Dolphin, he wondered why Henry had to choose so distant a tavern for his patronage. The streets were dark and warm, sliding untidily down the hill to the water, smelling of smoke and cooking and dirt. From the topmost chimneys one could see the sea beyond the grazing and the marshes, and the distant sail going down to London.

Matt had no trouble finding The Barge. It was the most popular of the smacksmen's haunts, in spite of the fact that it was farthest from the water, and tonight it was very much aware of the festive occasion, so much so that Matt could hardly fight his way inside. After the coolness of the dusking summer air outside, the interior of The Barge was like a furnace. The flaring bowls of the gas lamps swam mazily out of a mist of tobacco smoke and into this thick light laughter and argument trumpeted, tankards clattered on the counter, a piano tinkled. Matt squared his shoulders and struggled through the crush, hoping that his emblazoned jersey might stand him in good stead when he got to the counter. He was lucky, for the landlord himself caught sight of it and came over.

"The steward sent you up, eh? I've been so busy I couldn't spare the lad to take the brandy down. You wait here and I'll fetch it."

"There's ale as well," Matt said, and gave his message.

"Aye, you wait. I'll fetch it for you."

Matt, anchored now in his corner, put his back to the bar and surveyed the scene. The place was so noisy it made his head whirl. Beside him along the wall tables had been set up with big settles round them, and here there was much earnest talk going on. From the group right behind him he heard *Juno* mentioned, and then *Good Fortune*. Then, clearly out of the mumble of conservation, the phrase, "If *Juno* doesn't win, it will be the ruin of me."

In reply, low and firm, came the statement, "*Juno* will win. You rest assured."

The little drama happened very quickly. Matt, recognizing the voice, spun round in astonishment. A great shout of laughter from a party at the bar effectively drowned any more conversation, but Matt had no need to hear more. "*Juno* will win. You rest assured." The voice was Beckett's and as Matt turned he saw Beckett a table's width away, facing him across an array of bottles and glasses. As Matt turned, Beckett lifted his eyes, attracted by the laughter beyond. He was smiling, but he could not help but see Matt. Matt saw his expression change, saw a sudden, sober flash of fear cross his heavy features. Matt's own astonishment in the same moment turned to fear and for what seemed to him an eternity he stared at Beckett over the heads of his drinking companions like a mesmerized hare. The fact that Beckett, too, was frightened did not help him. He felt his heart thumping in the suffocating atmosphere and the sweat beading his lip. He thought Beckett was going to say something to him, but in the din he wouldn't have heard the words. With an effort he dragged his eyes away and turned back to the bar, praying for the landlord to bring his ale and brandy.

But the landlord was still down in his cellars, and Matt knew he was trapped. Beckett knew he had overheard that fateful phrase. *Juno* will win. *Juno*! The black traitor! Matt's head swam at the enormity of his knowledge. How much was *Juno*'s winning worth to Beckett? he wondered. A good sum, no doubt, enough to set him up for a few years. He would be paid well; it would mean more to him than the betrayal of his employer. And with his skill he had probably worked out a plan that would never give him away, a snapping sheet perhaps, or a broken forestay. The thoughts raced through Matt's head as he stared blindly across the counter, acutely aware now of his own danger in having this knowledge. The laughter and the noise and the smoky stinging light seemed to beat at him, and the strong pulses of fear throbbed through his body. Beckett, Beckett, *Beckett* he thought, clenching his hands on the wet counter. Always the man dogged him and each crisis in their lives was a crisis shared, and in their encounters it was Beckett who won, Beckett with his strength and his cunning and cruelty. Matt had no illusions about Beckett's next move. There was no one in this rowdy, drunken crowd he could turn to for help. He could only wait for the inevitable to happen, wait for the slender chance that would, if he were lucky, see him safely home.

Beckett was already up from his table and pushing his way roughly across the room. Matt watched him sharply, craning over the shoulders of his neighbors. He saw him speak to three youths standing near the door, raw-looking louts with red drunken eyes, who listened to him with eager attention. Matt thought some money changed hands; he saw Beckett point him out. He noticed that there was only one door out of the tavern, the one where the youths stood.

"Here's your drink, lad. The brandy's paid for." The landlord put four bottles of brandy on the counter and a big stone jar of ale. "You can just about manage it, I think."

"Your—your boy couldn't come with me?" Matt asked hesitantly.

The landlord gave him a strange look and said, "He's got too much to do. Saving your strength, are you?"

Matt flushed, and handed up Henry's purse. The landlord took the money, found an old sacking bag to put the brandy bottles in, and pushed the load over the counter. Matt swung the heavy jar in one hand and the bag in the other and automatically started to push his way out through the crowd. There was no sign now of either Beckett or the youths he had been talking to, but Matt felt no elation on that score. He shouldered his way roughly out into the street and stood for a moment in the pool of light beneath the creaking sign of the Thames barge in lurid sail that hung out over the cobbles. His first panicky fear had died down now, and it was with a sense of despair more than fright that he started off down the hill, a feeling of great loneliness. He would have given his new smack *Reward* at that moment to have had the cheerful bulk of George Firmin at his side. Somewhere behind him in the brilliantly lit hotel in the market square Mr. Shelley and Francis were entertaining their regatta guests, but Matt knew he stood as little chance of reaching them as he did the *Good Fortune*.

He set off down the hill. It was not yet very late and there were people about, but nobody Matt felt he wanted to beg help from. Besides, as he went on he saw no signs of pursuit and he wondered if perhaps he was dramatizing the incident a little. It helped to believe that, although he had no doubts in his heart. The ale was heavy and the bottles awkward, and his arms soon began to ache. The hill ran

down before him and he could see the masts of a schooner
tangled up with some chimneys and the wet gleam of a lamp
reflected in the water, and he thought of the little streets
that ran out onto the quays and the lonely road back to
Melville's. The night was very warm and he could smell the
river and the saltings there among the cobbles.

He was nearly at the bottom of the hill when he first
heard the three men behind him. He tightened his grip on
his load and quickened his step. For a moment he wondered
whether to drop everything and run for it, but when he
glanced over his shoulder again he saw that there was only
one boy, and he was confused. Had the other two ducked
into one of the alleys to overtake him and cut him off?
Side streets and alleys crisscrossed here at all angles. At
every black entrance Matt hesitated, and he felt the fear
mounting up again, not knowing whether to hurry or
whether to stop. The narrow streets were dismal and empty
and his footsteps echoed against warehouse walls, the dull
sound repeated a hundred paces back by the boy who followed him. He walked on reluctantly, his heart pounding.

Suddenly the two youths came out of a yard entrance just
ahead of him. Matt stopped dead. The footsteps behind him
quickened and the three boys converged on Matt together.
There was no way out for him, for there were brick walls on
both sides. So he put his back to the wall, dropped his stone
jar, and got a brandy bottle in each hand. He had just time
to take aim, and as the first boy leaped for him he swung
desperately. There was a crack and a groan and a stench
of spirits, but before he had time to raise the second one
Matt found himself on his back on the cobbles, rolling over
and over with a pair of hands trying to get a grip on his
throat. He slipped the grasp like an eel, but a boot came up
against his temple, almost stunning him. He heard a hoarse

voice in his ear and saw the coarse eager face of the drunken
lout swaying above him. Another boot landed in his ribs,
but he managed to roll over again and tip the youth with
him, and they were groveling once more with grunts and
curses. Dimly Matt realized that his adversaries were
clumsy with drink, and he fought like a cat to get free of
the oaf that hung onto him with mulish stubbornness. Boot
blows rained down on him, but his opponent received as
many as he did and presently Matt felt his grip loosening.

But at the same moment the youth with the boots
growled, "Here, I'll finish him!" and as the drunkard rolled
free, Matt saw the gleam of a knife above him. As the blade
lunged down, Matt flung himself desperately out of the
way, knocking the youth's feet from under him. He rolled
over again, desperate. He felt the sudden burning pain of the
knife in his arm, and cried out, but at the same time he

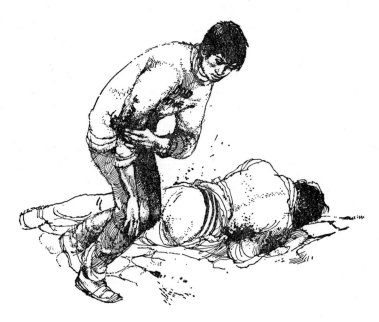

knew he was free. He lurched to his feet, stumbling over the prone body of the one he had felled with the brandy bottle and half-running, half-staggering, he headed for the quay and the glimmering light by the river. He made for his lair like a hunted fox, and his footsteps echoed wildly against the shuttered shops and offices, his shadow flaring on the walls. Some drunken fisherman jeered at him as he fled by and a cat hissed as it scuttered across his path but, gasping, he came at last to Melville's gate and staggered inside. The place was deserted, a faint breeze rustled up from the river, and below him he saw *Fathom* lying on the edge of the mud. He longed for the dark hole of her cuddy, but he knew that he would be found there, either by Beckett or by Henry, before the night was over. A place to lie in secret was all he wanted . . . His eyes roved across the yard and he saw his own smack *Reward*, her deck newly planked. With a feeling of great relief he limped over, climbed a saw bench onto her deck, and dropped down into her fo'c'sle. There were no floorboards in, but it didn't matter much. Nothing mattered save the safety of the darkness and the silence. He crouched down, clutching his pulsing arm through the blood-sodden sleeve of his jersey, and felt a great weariness flooding over him so that he could scarcely hold his head up any longer. He was too tired to be frightened, too tired to think, or scarcely to remember what had happened. He lay against the strong ribs of his new smack and felt the darkness come down.

Good *Fortune*'s Race

Matt never forgot the pain and the misery of the endless hours that followed. Afraid to move from his hiding place for fear of Beckett, he lay among the wood shavings, clutching his wounded arm, and wept at his defeat. He knew Beckett would be looking for him if he knew that he had got away with his life, and he no longer felt like maintaining his stubborn indifference to all that Beckett had done to him. He wanted to give in. His head throbbed and waves of sickness kept shaking him. All the wrongs and the humiliations he had suffered at Beckett's hands seemed to rise up through his nausea, and there was not one single victory of his own to put against them. At times half conscious, Matt felt he was being swamped not by physical exhaustion but by failure, failure so absolute that it had taken on the power to suck him dry of all resolution. Tomorrow, when it was light and the danger was past, he would go home. No one would hear what he had overheard. It was no business of his any more.

He slept dreamlessly, and woke up in the small hours, wracked with cramp and what seemed a multitude of pains. The agony was too much to endure; *Reward*'s ribs were like daggers along his spine. He struggled to his feet and with

169

an immense effort climbed onto a saw bench and put his head out of the hatch.

It was almost dawn. The air was still and clear and cold. The two big yachts, so soon to be all action, lay motionless at their moorings, spars and rigging engraved on a mother-of-pearl sky. Quite near on the water's edge *Fathom* lay. Her homely familiar shape gave Matt his first crumb of comfort. The cold air bathed his face; his eyes went from *Fathom* back to the slender yacht beyond. It was as if the two boats symbolized his choice, waiting to claim him, *Fathom* to take him home, *Good Fortune* to test him. It seemed at that moment very easy to go home. A few hours ago he thought he had made the decision. He had only to walk across the yard, go aboard, and break out the anchor. The tide would take the smack clear; a few minutes would see her out of sight of the yachts, the Shelleys, and the Becketts.

"So what are you waiting for?" Matt said to himself. He felt strangely irresolute.

He climbed out of the hatch and walked dizzily down the yard to the water's edge. He felt very weak and in the gray light he could see that the sleeve of his new jersey was sodden and dark with blood. His arm had no feeling in it at all. He managed to scull out to the smack with his sound arm and scramble aboard. He made the skiff fast and went up forward to the anchor chain, and there he hesitated. It wasn't the difficulty of getting the chain up that stopped him, but the bows of the *Good Fortune* across the water. Her stem rose up out of the water like a white lily, as shapely a line as Matt thought he had ever seen. The sight of it stopped him in his tracks.

"So *Juno*'s going to win, is she?" he said to himself.

What if he didn't go home? There would be no necessity to tell Mr. Shelley what he had overheard; he had only to turn up on board and Beckett would not dare to lose the race. Beckett would have reason to be afraid for once in his life. And afterwards . . . Matt gave a small shrug. A few hours ago he had been searching his mind in vain for a victory to chalk up against Beckett. He had one within his grasp now, if he wanted it.

He did not hesitate for long.

"All right, Mr. Beckett!" The sun was picking out the yacht's gilt work, and a milky-golden mist was smoking off the water. He did not have much time. The hands would soon be stirring, and Matt did not want to be seen yet awhile, least of all by Beckett. Just let him wait! Matt thought with a vicious satisfaction. I'll show him I'm not dead yet, not by a long chalk. He'll be sorry Henry ever sent me up to The Barge last night. What Henry would have to say about his precious brandy Matt did not stop to think.

He dropped down into *Fathom*'s cuddy and stripped off the filthy, once-white jersey. His old blue one was in a locker along with his best white shirt, which he was soon slitting into strips for bandages. The cut in his arm just below the shoulder was wide and ugly. He washed it hastily with fresh water out of the cask and bound it tightly together with the shirt, pulling the knots tight with his teeth. Rooting about some more, he found half a loaf of bread and some cheese which he ate ravenously and washed down with several mouthfuls of rum. Then, anxious that his skiff shouldn't be spotted and his presence suspected, he sculled hurriedly back to Melville's yard. *Reward* had served him well as a hiding place so far, and he reckoned she would do him now. He flung out his kedge and slipped back into her bare cuddy.

The next few hours passed like days. Matt tried not to

think, for he had an idea that his situation would not bear much examination, but it was hard to disregard the fact that he had just escaped death by a matter of inches, and was more than likely to face it again if Beckett had his way. He stared steadily at the frames of his new smack, lit dimly by the golden wires of light quivering through her uncaulked seams. Should he have gone home? he wondered.

"It's too late now," he told himself savagely, nursing his heavy arm. "What's the use of thinking about it?"

The yard gate slammed and he heard the sound of voices. They went by down the yard. Soon there were others and footsteps hurrying along the street outside, and the excited laughter of Melville's apprentices as they ragged each other by the water. Even in his hiding place he could sense the excitement.

Beckett will be feeling pleased with himself by now, Matt thought. It's time I was going.

He got cautiously to his feet, praying that he would find the strength to see him through the day. His arm felt very strange, but otherwise he seemed to have recovered from the worst effects of his fight. The dizziness had gone, and the effort to climb out of the hatch was much less exhausting than before. Encouraged, Matt slithered down to the ground and made for the water.

Several rowing boats were gilling about at the edge and Matt hailed the nearest and asked to be taken out to the *Good Fortune*. On board the yacht he could see plenty of activity going on. Dinghies and rowing boats buzzed round her, hooters and whistles echoed from the crowded wharves, and hosts of little boys darted along the water's edge like scuttling crabs, shrieking cheeky advice to all within sight.

"A bit late if you're one of the crew, aren't you?" Matt's

pilot remarked slyly as he rowed him out across the tide. "Got into a bit of mischief last night, eh?"

Matt nodded, wondering just how disheveled he looked. But it was too late for worrying any longer. The boat went alongside *Good Fortune*'s counter, and with a suffocating nervousness pulsing in his breast Matt swung out with his good arm and scrambled up on deck.

Beckett was standing by the tiller with his back to him, talking to Mr. Shelley. Francis was there, too, listening to the conversation, and it was he who saw Matt first.

"Matt!" he cried. "Wherever have you been?"

Beckett swung round like a shying horse. In that moment Matt was able to savor Beckett's dismay to the full, for he was too startled to hide his alarm. The florid color drained out of his face; his black eyes flicked Matt's face like daggers. He said nothing after his first gasp, but Matt saw his hands tremble on the tiller as Shelley turned. But Matt's moment of triumph was short-lived, too, for Mr. Shelley's eyes were equally eloquent, although of a different emotion.

"So you've decided to join us, I see," he said coolly.

His eyes raked Matt from top to toe. It was only Matt's own knowledge that he was, in fact, blameless that allowed him to meet the gaze without flinching, but he felt his color rising at Shelley's contempt.

"Yes, sir."

"Might I ask why you never came back last night, and what became of the goods you were sent to buy?"

"I bought the goods, sir," Matt said steadily. "Mr. Beckett can testify to that."

"Mr. Beckett?"

"Yes, sir. He was in The Barge when I bought them."

"Er—yes, that's right, sir," Beckett mumbled after an in-

quiring gaze from his employer. His black eyes were fixed
on Matt's face. Matt could see the fear rising, quivering in
Beckett's face.

"And why did you not bring them back?"

"I—I was attacked, sir, and the bottles were broken."

"Why did you not come back and tell Henry last night?"

Matt did not reply. He had said enough to frighten
Beckett out of his wits, and that was all he wanted, whatever Mr. Shelley's conclusions might be.

"A drunken brawl, I suppose," Shelley commented. "At
least you can prove it by your appearance."

He reached out and none too gently pushed Matt's hair
back off his forehead, where a purple bruise was spreading,
flecked with dried blood. Matt winced, and Shelley dropped
his arm with a slight shrug of resignation. Matt sensed
that he was disappointed, and he was sorry, bitterly sorry,
but there was nothing he could do about it. Francis was
looking at him strangely, too, with a slightly wary look in
his eyes, as if he had suddenly seen him in a new light.

"I'll speak to you after the race," Mr. Shelley said sharply.
"I hope you are fit enough to do your duty, that's all."

Matt was hoping very much the same thing as he went
forward with the rest of the hands to get the mainsail up.
His mind was confused now, his feelings a mixture of jubi-
lation at Beckett's shock and contrition towards his employer who thought he had failed him. He knew he had
effectively checked any plans Beckett had had for throwing
away the race, but Mr. Shelley's look of contempt had hurt
Matt more than he had anticipated.

His part in getting the sails up was nearly a match for
Matt, but as the pain in his arm threatened to overcome him,
he set his teeth and with each pull forced himself to remember: There's only one mainsail to get up. The high-peaked

gaff slipped idly, surely, up against the flawless blue sky, quivering to the wind like a gull's wing. The big yacht was suddenly restive to her anchor chain, responsive to the life in the great spreading flood of her sail, so that now everyone had a mind only for the ship, for nursing her off her mooring into a river that suddenly seemed too small to hold her. Ripples of excitement broke out along the shore as the anchor started to grate in over the bows. *Juno* was already away, but there was almost an hour yet to go to the start, which was taking place down on the river mouth. The flotilla of small boats that lined the river was setting off to accompany them. Cheers and sirens echoed across the water and small sails darted about like butterflies, scurrying clear as the yacht's anchor broke out and the impatient sails filled.

The weather for the day of the regatta was as perfect as anyone in Marchester could have desired: a day of stately white cloud and azure sky, the wind perhaps a trifle light, but promising more strength as the day went on. As the *Good Fortune* heeled away, close-hauled, down the river after *Juno*, her hands were busy getting her in racing trim, jib and topsail ready to go up when there was sea room to luff up into the wind. Beckett, his hand clenched on the tiller, missed nothing, from the set of *Juno*'s sails ahead of him to the sweat of pain on Matt's face. Mr. Shelley stood just behind him with Francis and two of his friends, apparently full of sporting *joie de vivre*. But there was a deadly seriousness in his eye.

Down at the river mouth the starter's boat was anchored in line with the buoys that marked the start, and around it a host of smacks, rowing boats, and dinghies lay at anchor or laced dangerously in and out across the tide. On the shore shouting children ran barefoot up and down the beach, and the saltings were fringed with an excited crowd out for the day with picnic hampers and straw hats, whistles and hooters. Somewhere over there, Matt knew, his mother was standing with Anne, the baby on her shoulder. He was only thankful she knew nothing of his recent adventures. He crouched down on the deck when all the sails were set and fixed his dizzy eyes on the horizon seaward, praying to find his second wind before they went over the line. He felt desperately weak again; whether it was apparent to Mr. Shelley he could not tell, although he knew Beckett must have noticed. The weakness angered him, for now he wanted to forget his own troubles and concentrate on helping *Good Fortune* to win. This was to be the race of her life. Already the wind had freshened in her sails down here on the threshold of the open sea and she was creaming along across the river as if she could not wait to get away.

To see how she looked, Matt only had to glance across the water to *Juno*, who was going past them on the other tack, her narrow bows throwing up a flurry of spray which seemed to melt into the white press of her sail. She was an awe-inspiring sight, and Matt knew that the *Good Fortune* was looking every bit as fine under her straining topsails, that they were as evenly matched as it was possible for two yachts to be, and that a great deal would depend on skippers and crews to decide the issue.

The five-minute gun boomed across the water and, at minute intervals, further explosions set the crowd cheering with excitement and the crews tense by the sheets. A good start was imperative. Beckett seemed to know exactly what he wanted to do, and the judgment with which he put his yacht to windward of *Juno* right on the line as the gun fired brought a hysterical cheer of appreciation from across the river. Even Matt smiled at the beauty of the maneuver: The *Good Fortune* was away three clear lengths ahead.

There was no doubt in Matt's mind now that Beckett intended the *Good Fortune* to win. The yacht stood out to sea, reveling in the fresh breeze that came to her as the shoreline fell away. Visibility was so good that the buoy marking the first leg of the race could be seen with the naked eye, a distant speck through the sparkling mist of the spray over the bows. The sea was white-crested right to the horizon, the deep troughs of the waves sapphire-dark and laced with foam from the yacht's passage. *Juno* was at the *Good Fortune*'s heels, neither gaining nor losing as the minutes passed, and the tension mounted as the buoy came nearer. On the second leg of the race the wind would be dead ahead, and the pattern was likely to change as the yachts started beating.

"Ready—about!"

To Matt the race was two hours of the most confused emotions, of nerve-wracking exhilaration and tension, of gripping excitement interspersed with stumbling, witless periods when he hardly knew what he was doing at all. It was a confusion of merciless sheet-trimming to the thunder and roar of the sea under the lee rail, with the vision of *Juno* like a shadow unleashed falling away or plunging past on the opposite tack. Water scoured the decks continually; occasionally there was a brief, damp breather crouched on the weather side of a hatch cover; then with the roar of "Lee-oh!" the boom would rattle across again and the sheets would fly and be captured by burning hands, secured with curses, until Beckett would roar for an inch more out, or a foot or two more in, which meant all six to a haul that left Matt faint with the pain in his arm. He would turn his face to the reviving spray and the *Good Fortune* would leap under his feet. The whole pattern would be repeated: "Lee-oh!" and the convulsed sheets whipped through their leads, the sails refilling with an eagerness that threatened to tear them apart.

Francis, sprawling on the deck aft with his father and the two breathless guests, thrilled to the performance of the yacht with an ecstasy he had never known before. He saw the handling of the two yachts not as a race, but as a sort of complex choreography to an orchestra of wind and water. *Juno* with her raking sails and crystal cloud of spray was the loveliest, most cruelly strong and powerful machine he had ever seen. With his eyes on the rival, his body and ears attuned to the movement of the ship beneath him, he sensed that he was experiencing the very essence of all a sailing ship had to offer, primed to the peak of her performance. He was not worried about his father's thousand pounds; he had no part in the physical exertions of the crew nor the responsibility of the helmsman. He was just a sponge absorbing smell and scene and wishing it could last forever.

As the two yachts rounded the second buoy *Good Fortune* was still ahead by about fifty yards. Mr. Shelley was tense, his lips clipped tight.

"Haul in your mainsheet!" Beckett was roaring, and the yacht surged ahead on the squally beam wind, heading back to the river. *Juno*, a swathe of white under her bows, was racing along to windward, but was still unable to touch the tumbling wake of her adversary. Small, excited sails were beating out of the river to meet them, and a thread of frenzied cheering frightened the ducks across the saltings so that they whirred up against the sky. Beckett's hand was like a rock on the helm and Matt knew that the *Good Fortune* was invincible. No one could sail a boat like Beckett, be what he may. Matt's heart was pounding with pride and excitement as the little pilot boats fluttered about to cheer them home and *Juno*, as if discouraged, lost another length. And even Beckett, with his intentions reversed and the race won which he had wanted to lose, had a light of triumph in his eye, for the victory after a hard race was too fine to leave him unmoved. Mr. Shelley's face was red with excitement and his friends were shaking his hand as they went over the line.

The race secured, the *Good Fortune* brought down her topsails and after an exchange of courtesies with *Juno* and the dignitaries of Marchester on a barge beside the starter she headed back up the river towards her mooring. Mr. Shelley and his friends went below for a celebration, and the crew hustled round tidying up the decks. Now that the excitement was over, Beckett was obviously remembering what the win had cost him and he stood glowering at them, barking orders savagely as he put the yacht about to keep her in deep water. Matt was anxious to get onto *Fathom*, for he had to sail downstream with a foul tide to get her onto the starting line, and if the wind veered, it might take an hour or so. Fortunately Beckett was in the same situation and was not wasting any time. It was only the knowledge that there was another race to be won that kept Matt going at all, for his head was spinning and he felt sick and spent. But only complete loss of consciousness would have stopped him.

The anchor was dropped to the cheers of another enthusiastic crowd, and a flotilla of admirers flocked round as the yacht's sails were stowed and decks cleaned. Mr. Shelley appeared on deck to announce that Henry had refreshment for the crew below, and Beckett excused himself, received a congratulatory handshake from his employer, and slipped down into the rowing boat his brother had waiting for him. Matt stepped forward anxiously.

"Excuse me, sir."

To his relief Francis cut in. "Father, Matt is racing his smack, too. You promised I could go with him. May we go now?"

Mr. Shelley hesitated and gave Matt a searching look.

"He looks more to me as if he could do with sleeping off the effects of his evening's entertainment," he said coldly. "But I suppose I cannot stop you. I will see you after the race, Matt."

"Yes, sir."

"I'll wish you good luck, too. You did well this morning, in spite of your—er—infirmities."

He almost smiled.

Matt's heart lifted at this unexpected forgiveness. "Thank you, sir," he said.

Mr. Shelley turned and tossed a coin into the nearest boat. "Take these lads up to the smack off Melville's," he ordered, and in a minute Matt and Francis were heading for *Fathom*, glancing at each other with a new excitement.

Fathom's Last Sail

This was going to be different, Matt knew, as he looked towards *Fathom*'s stocky mast. He glanced at Francis doubtfully, but Francis was smiling with a quiet anticipation. On his lap he nursed a big bundle wrapped in white cloth.

"I've brought some of the celebrations with me," he explained, catching Matt's eyes. "I didn't see why we should go without."

Matt felt much better at the sight of the crackling linen provided by the meticulous Henry.

"This race won't be quite the same as this morning's," he said, looking up at *Fathom* as they drew near. "She's a far cry from the *Good Fortune*."

"It might be a good race though," Francis said. "Melville seems to have a good opinion of her."

"Aye, she's fast as smacks go. We might win." But Matt did not dare think that he would.

They landed on board. Matt went to the mast and took the topping lift, and sent Francis forward to the anchor. But the spar felt to Matt as if it were made of solid lead and, with twenty-five pounds at stake, he felt obliged to ask Francis for a hand to get the sail up taut.

"What's wrong—with—with you?" Francis panted as he swung down on the halyard. "Where did—you get to last night?"

"I was mixed up in a fight. I told your father the truth. I hurt my arm, that's all."

Matt did not want Francis to think badly of him, but it was an impossible story to explain without telling of Beckett's treachery. Matt guessed that Francis thought he had got drunk, as most smacksmen did on regatta nights, but he had no way of proving otherwise. Francis cleated home the halyard and looked at him doubtfully.

"I don't mind doing the heaving and hauling if I can," he said. "You're sure you're all right—to go—I mean?"

"Yes, of course," Matt said impatiently. "I'll be better when I've got some of Henry's celebrations inside me, too. Come on, break out that anchor, else we'll miss the start."

Charity was already disappearing round the bend downstream, having been sailed up to meet her skipper, but in a few minutes *Fathom* was following her, her heavy sails taut in the wind. Matt could feel the difference they made, and a pulse of optimism flickered in his breast. He had beaten Beckett once today; perhaps this was his second chance. Francis had broken into Henry's gleaming parcel, and Matt devoured everything he was offered with undisguised enthusiasm, feeling his strength come back as cheese and ham on crusty fresh bread filled the empty regions of his stomach. The wind had been freshening steadily since the morning, and as *Fathom* reached down the river Matt felt for the first time, with his new-found strength, that the old smack might win. At least there were no mysteries among his adversaries; the Marshfield smacks held no secrets from each other. Matt knew he could beat most of them, but there were a few, like *Charity* and the cleverly sailed

Miranda, which might prove his match. And the fact that there were only two of them aboard wouldn't help.

"I wonder if the twins . . ." he murmured under his breath. As they sailed down the last reach and saw the fleet of smacks gilling about near the start, Matt put *Fathom* about for the lee shore, where the crowds were working up a fresh—and more personal—excitement for the start of the local race.

"If my brothers are there, they'd do to help crew," he said to Francis. "They're only young, but they'd know what they were doing. We'll see if we can pick them up."

The beach shelved steeply and he was able to sail close. The twins quickly made themselves conspicuous by their wildly waving arms and yells of recognition and one of the spectator's boats soon picked them up when Matt made known what he wanted. They were put aboard breathless with excitement, wriggling with awe at sight of Francis, speechless at Matt's stern demeanor.

"I'm not taking you for the ride," he told them briskly. "You're coming to work, and just you keep your ears open and your wits about you and do exactly what you're told else I'll put the belt about you just like your father did to me. There's twenty-five pounds in this race for us if we win, and God knows we could use it."

The twins, flushed and solemn, nodded gravely. They got down on the deck, one by each jib sheet, and *Fathom* went creaming across the river to join the mêlée on the line. Matt was praying he might, when the time came, make as sweet a start as Beckett had made in the *Good Fortune,* but if he did, he thought it would be more by good luck than good judgment. Quite a number of the smacks had decided that the wind was too strong to carry a topsail, but the two smacks that stood most chance of winning, *Charity* and

Miranda, had all sail up, like *Fathom.* The sky was full of clouds now, purple-shadowed, fleeting over the sun, so that the water darkened and shone alternately. Matt knew it would be a fast, wet race, hard on poor old *Fathom,* for he did not intend to spare her.

"That's the five-minute gun," Francis said, as a shot echoed over the water. He pulled his watch out of his pocket.

"I'll be lucky if I get away like Beckett did," said Matt. "We'll do our best, though."

As the minutes passed, the smacks maneuvered cunningly off the starter's barge. Matt took *Fathom* clear and as the last minute ticked away to the gun he sheeted her hard and sailed her fast for the line. Francis bit his lip, his eyes on the watch. The second hand crawled round as *Fathom* hissed ahead with a plume of spray at her bows.

"How are we?" Matt muttered anxiously.

"Twenty seconds to go . . . fifteen . . ."

Matt eased the sheet a fraction. If he was lucky, he would cross the line on the gun to a flying start; if he had misjudged his speed, he would cross it too soon and be recalled.

"Ten . . . you'll be all right," Francis murmured. He glanced round. *Charity* was immediately behind them. If *Fathom* crossed the line before the gun, it would be by half a second! The two boys, white-faced, strained their ears for the shot as *Fathom* bore down on the line.

"Too soon!" Matt breathed, in agony.

"No! She's fine!"

A puff of blue smoke went up from the starter's barge, followed by the report of the gun and a simultaneous roar from the crowd ashore. *Fathom* was first over, and traveling her fastest.

"Wonderful! Even better than Beckett!" Francis cried,

and the two boys grinned at each other with pride. Matt felt like throwing his cap in the air and cheering, and the twins were up on their feet and capering again. He shouted at them from the helm and set his course for the first buoy.

"Slacken your sheet a foot, Jack! Get down, Joe, you fool! If you go overboard, we're not stopping!"

The tide was on the turn, slack as the small fleet of smacks spend out of the river. Their course lay round the river-mouth buoy, before the wind to the Marshfield creek, round the boat that had been moored there for the occasion, and a beat back to the river. Then a mile up the estuary against a foul tide to the finishing line. Matt wondered how *Fathom* would stand it. One of his chief reasons for getting the twins on board was to have a spare hand to work the pump should the occasion arise, which he guessed it would.

The water was rough once out of the shelter of the river. As she reached for the buoy the water streamed through *Fathom*'s scuppers. She still led, with *Charity* right behind her and a group of three, including *Miranda*, following fairly closely.

"We'll have to jibe her round the buoy. Get ready to pull in the mainsheet," Matt said. "Watch the jib sheet, Joe, and be ready to let it go."

As the black buoy slipped past a yard off their starboard bow, Francis hauled frantically on the mainsheet. Matt ducked under the boom and put the helm over.

"Let it go! Let it go!"

The twins were scurrying across the deck to make fast their respective sheets, and in a moment *Fathom* was running for Marshfield, the big waves running beside her with their tops curling, occasionally lifting her by the stern and rolling beneath her with a surge which rattled the topsail. The motion was violent and the twins braced themselves against the mast, watching the sea with wide, respectful eyes. *Charity*'s bows were alongside and Beckett's brothers braced on her streaming decks, each one three times as big as *Fathom*'s jib-hands, their dark faces insolent and confident as they stared at the smack alongside. Beckett on the helm kept his eyes on the sails.

"She'll beat us running," Matt said to Francis as *Charity* gradually slipped past. "But we might catch up coming back. We'll be beating back, and *Fathom*'s quick in stays."

But he did not want to see *Charity* get too far ahead. He had his mainsail out as far as it would go, and as the wind came dead aft, he got the staysail and jib out goose-winged so that *Fathom* rolled down the sea like a seagull on the wind. Getting neatly onto the foam of *Charity*'s wake, he effectively took most of Beckett's wind and by the time they got to the Marshfield creek *Charity* was no more than fifty yards ahead, and *Fathom* was still lying comfortably ahead of *Miranda* and the rest.

"Now we'll feel it," Matt said as the moored boat slipped towards them. "It'll be hard work going back."

The twins jumped to their sheets as Matt put the helm over to round the mark. As soon as they had cleared it the motion aboard *Fathom* changed abruptly. With the mainsail sheeted in once more, she leaped into the breakers that had previously rolled her with them, tossing them aside in sheets of spray so that her bows seemed to disappear altogether. The deck was a streaming mass of water, the weather rigging wire-taut. Matt, his eyes on the worn sheets, prayed that nothing would give. *Charity* still had her topsail up, and while that was ahead of him to act as goad, Matt knew he would never bring himself to take in his own, even if *Fathom*'s old hull cracked under the strain. Even on the first board out to sea Matt knew she was making water through

her stem, and he put Jack on the pump to keep the level
in the bilges down. Francis, his hair hanging in wet curls
over his forehead, his sodden shirt clinging to him, took
Jack's place on the jib, grinning back at Matt as *Fathom*
threshed her way ahead. The sun, gleaming momentarily
far out at sea, was continually swallowed up by chasing,
towering clouds; wild shadows flew over the shore, veiling
the bright pools in the mud and the pink fringes of sea

lavender. Matt, determined and anxious, forced the tiller over with his thigh, cursing the weakness that hampered him. Jack labored on the pump, panting, and *Fathom* plunged on. Matt did not ease her by an inch. *Charity*'s topsail was still up, and Matt knew *Fathom* was holding *Charity*.

They went about and Joe changed places with Jack on the pump. Peering through the hatch as he gave up his place, Jack saw the gleam of water sloshing over the cuddy floor below and said, "It doesn't seem to make much difference."

"She's all right," Matt said shortly.

Miranda was close on their tail, but Matt did not think she would pass unless he blundered. But if *Charity* got away now, he knew they would never catch her again. The big smack was sailing hard, but she was not as quick going about as *Fathom*, and Matt was encouraged when he saw Beckett glance over his shoulder once or twice.

"We'll catch her! We'll catch her!" the twins were chanting, ducking their heads as the sails cracked over. Francis, deft on the sheets, made them fast and ran back to help Matt trim the mainsheet. On the fourth board, going about sooner than *Charity*, *Fathom* drew level. Francis glanced at Matt's tense face.

"Do you think we can keep ahead of her?"

Matt squinted through the spray to catch sight of the rivermouth buoy again. "We'll round it first, but she'll catch us up the river," he said.

"She might split a sail or something," Francis said.

"So might we," Matt said, with the hint of a smile. "We might split our hull, too. Take a turn on the pump—Joe's failing."

At times *Fathom*'s deck was hardly distinguishable from the sea itself. Matt knew the old smack had never taken such a beating, not even the night they went out to the wreck when she had, at least, been sailed with consideration. If he had had another winter to go in her, he knew he would have run down his topsail and conceded to *Charity* long ago, but with the vision of the new smack fresh in his mind he was determined to sail her to her limit. Old she might be, but she was a nimble girl, and Matt's heart warmed to her courage as the seas came running over her decks and she rose up clear, throwing them off and shouldering her way forward, slicing the dark sea with her stem. In spite of the pumping, Matt sensed that there was more water in her bilges than suited her, but he hoped she would stop taking it in once they rounded the buoy again.

On their next board they made the buoy and rounded it several lengths ahead of *Charity*. Matt trimmed his sheets and set his course into the river and knew there was no more he could do. A glance over his shoulder showed him *Charity* coming round in a flurry of spray, the brothers throwing their brute strength onto the sheets, making fast and grinning into the wind. They were not afraid of *Fathom*'s lead, as Matt knew they had no reason to be. The big smack bit into the ebbing tide, powerful and tireless, and Matt watched her black bows drawing nearer, the jib pulling like an eager horse in its traces. Francis gave Matt a despairing look.

"What can we do? She can't beat us now!"

Matt could feel the disappointment flooding through him, in spite of the fact that things were only turning out as he had predicted. His eyes stubborn and angry, he watched *Charity* draw up, remembering the times she had raced his father when their holds were full and how his father had glared at those same powerful bows, turning up a bow wave like a revenue cutter after a smuggler.

There was a mile to go yet, round the long bend of the

river where the deep channel made a dog's leg detour to clear the notorious Butler's spit, a hard shoal which stuck out like a bar from the left-hand bank, and then up the home straight where the faithful fleet of spectators was already waiting, along with the Mayor's barge and the shore contingent who had all moved upriver for the finish. Matt knew that he would be second, should *Fathom* hold together that long, but he might as well be last as second, for he was not interested in the honor and glory this time, but only in the prize.

Beckett was sailing close-hauled now, to clear the spit. He was well clear of *Fathom*, and as the wind gusted up the river Matt heard him shout to one of his brothers. The next moment *Charity*'s topsail was handed, and this insolent show of confidence goaded Matt beyond endurance. So Beckett thought he had won already! Matt's eyes went desperately to the withies that marked the spit, checking the height of the ebb. If there was water enough over it, he'd beat Beckett yet, or wreck *Fathom* in the attempt!

It was no good explaining to Francis. Matt knew he had nothing to lose, and he gave the tiller an inch with his thigh to head his bows towards the line of withies. The twins stared at him.

"What are we doing?"

"We'll try and get over the spit. It's the only way we can beat him. Pull your sheet in and keep your fingers crossed."

Fathom raced on to the confused line of water ahead of her where the ebb was pouring out over the bar of silted mud. The wind was strong, gusting on her beam, and Matt thought she might do it. The ebb was only a couple of hours old. But his heart was pounding as the withies slid towards them. Francis had said nothing, but he stopped work on the pump, and there was a doubtful frown between his eyes.

Some of the more observant of the spectator fleet who had
spotted the rash intentions of the lonely sail were already
scurrying downstream to watch the fun, and Matt could
sense Beckett's eyes on him across the widening stretch of
water between them—anxious, he hoped. As anxious as his
own probably. The first withy slid past their boom end, and
the yellow water came at them in angry broken waves.
Fathom rolled and her boom swung dangerously; her jib
flapped and filled again with a report like gunshot. She was
traveling fast in spite of the ebb against her, but the color of
the water showed how close the bottom was. Halfway across
she bumped, and Matt's heart lurched with her. The crash
and slew, and crash again, was physical pain to Matt, and
his hand clenched with anguish on the tiller.

"Come on, *Fathom*, come on!" he breathed.

She lifted and sailed again and then a sickening jar
brought her up all standing, sails and spars rattling desperately. Matt heard the cracking of timber, and as the sweat
came out on his forehead, he saw the wind slam into the
mainsail again as if it would tear it to ribbons. The boom
flew out again with a jerk that nearly snapped the sheet, and
by a miracle *Fathom* was lifting again and stumbling on,
lifting and bumping like a one-legged man across the seething water. Matt breathed encouragement to her, nursing her
sheet and praying as he had never prayed before. Her press
of sail was laying her down. Her lee deck was right under,
but it was this that was helping her keel to clear the bottom.

"She's across! She's across!" Francis was muttering, as if
to convince himself. He had never experienced the agony of
a grounding ship before, and the bumps wrenched him with
the same pity Matt felt for his smack. He clutched the
pump handle as if he would lift the boat bodily, and winced
as the shock came up through the soles of his feet.

"She won't stand much of this," Matt said, white-faced. But the fact that she was still moving gave him a shred of hope. She was well across the spit now and still tearing herself forward as each wave lifted her. *Charity* was just rounding the end of the spit, frantically resetting her topsail. If *Fathom* came off now, she would be ahead of Beckett by at least a hundred yards.

"Start pumping," Matt shouted to Francis. "I think she's coming!"

Even as she shook herself free at last, Matt knew the old smack was mortally wounded. He had no need to look through the hatch to know that the lake in the cuddy was rising fast. Sluggishly he felt her pick up speed and, close-hauled, thresh her way home up the river, pitching and pounding and rolling, with the water oozing up through every cracked seam below, swilling into her lockers like a ballast of loose sprats. She was well clear of *Charity*, but settling in the water with each length she sailed. The twins watched her diminishing freeboard with hypnotized eyes while Francis sweated hopelessly over the pump. The dinghies were all about them, and there was not a man in them but was cheering the old smack home, willing her to hold the fast-approaching *Charity*. The finishing mark looked to Matt's weary eyes a hopeless distance away, but his hand was clenched on the tiller; he wasn't showing *Fathom* mercy now. Somehow she was stemming this eager tide, the water streaming through her planks, and still *Charity* was astern of her. The roaring on the shore was all for *Fathom*, and if the crowd could have lifted her up on its voice, it would have done, for her courage had won them over completely.

Francis glanced round desperately. Matt's face was taut with strain. *Charity* was sailing up behind them with a great flush of foam at her bows, the dark-faced brothers swearing from her deck. Somehow *Fathom* still stemmed the tide, and the finishing line by a miracle was sliding towards them, but right until the last Matt thought it was meeting them too late. With the roars of the crowd gusting and shrilling on the wind all round her, *Fathom* rolled past the vital barge, and Matt saw Beckett's black face alongside, and the veins standing out in his neck with pure rage. Even then, with *Charity*'s long bowsprit raking out ahead, Matt did not know who had won. He was looking to the shore to put *Fathom*'s split ribs on the mud for the last time and his emotions had drained away to a numb pity for his doomed boat. She was foundering beneath them, her boom skimming the wave-tops, her transom with the carved name-letters settling lower and lower with each roll. The spectator fleet crowded her flanks like mourners to a funeral, silent now, anxious to see the smack make her landfall.

Matt chose his spot on a narrow outfall and, at last, eased the mainsheet. "Hold on," he said quietly, and *Fathom* grounded, burying her gaping seams into the mud that would hold her now until she rotted to splinters.

Matt Goes Home

They stood on the shore as the yellow tide ebbed away. Matt wished everyone would leave them alone, but a curious, admiring crowd was pressing round on all sides. Matt caught sight of some Marshfield boys and asked them who had won, and the boys stared at him and said, "You did, of course."

Matt expected to feel elated, but somehow he only felt numb and shocked, rather as he had felt after his father had been drowned. He could not take his eyes off poor old *Fathom* lying there with her sails shaken down and trailing over her decks, the water seeping out of her gaping seams as if it were her lifeblood draining away. He had never expected her to go like this, noble an end as it was. His legs felt heavy and he no longer knew what to do. He just stood looking at the pathetic rags of caulking hanging in tarry ribbons on the upturned bilge, wishing everyone would go away.

Francis said gently, "We'll get Melville's sails off her, shall we? Perhaps someone will take them up the river for us."

Matt looked up and nodded. "Yes, we must strip her, I suppose. There won't be much left on her by morning if we leave her to the sharks."

Marchester was full of "foreigners" who, he knew, would not hesitate to take a souvenir with them when they sailed for home. But as he stirred himself to start work on the old hull he saw George Firmin rowing towards him in a borrowed boat from the anchored *Miranda*, and presently the Firmin brothers were doing his work for him, handing the sails, unreeving the rigging, throwing blocks and fittings into a sack. They were jubilant at Matt's win and richly satisfied with Beckett's defeat. Francis joined in happily, as if he had been a smacksman all his life, and in a minute

Matt found himself blindly helping with the butchery. He loaded a bundle of warps into the skiff that George and Clem had pulled up the mud, and was gathering together his stow net when he saw his mother and Anne standing there with the baby, their faces a mixture of dismay and excitement.

"You won, Matt!" Mary Pullen cried when she saw him. "But poor old *Fathom*! I never thought I'd see her like this!"

"It's all right, Mother. The next smack will be ready soon, and we've won the twenty-five pounds to go towards her."

His own words comforted Matt suddenly as he stood there on the mud. *Fathom* might be a carcass, but up the river the new smack was ready in her cradle of shavings, as strong and lovely as *Fathom* had been fifty years ago. He smiled for the first time.

"She's gone in a good cause, Mother," he said.

"Yes, you're right. You sailed a fine race, Matt, and I'm proud of you," Mary Pullen replied. "I'll feel happier when you're sailing on a sound boat. These five winters past have been nothing but anxiety."

Her eyes rested reflectively on her son's bruised face, but in front of his companions she said nothing. She hitched her skirts up out of the water and turned to follow the crowd that was now trailing back up the shore to the farm carts that waited to carry them up to Marchester for the evening's entertainments. Anne lingered for a moment. Her cheeks were pink with excitement, her heavy dark hair disheveled with the wind.

"It was wonderful, Matt! Beating Beckett. You were splendid!" She hesitated. "Have—have you been fighting?"

"Anne!" her mother called.

With a last anxious, excited glance at her brother Anne turned obediently away, hurrying across the shore.

Fathom lay stripped. Her spars were lashed down on *Miranda*'s deck, her coverless hatches gaped. Matt went down into the cuddy and rescued the old kettle and the tools and tarbrushes in her lockers. The blood-stained *Good Fortune* jersey he hid in a piece of old sacking and tucked under his arm. They carried these last bits and pieces down the shore and went aboard the now cluttered *Miranda*. A flotilla of sails and skiffs, of smacks, barges, and rowing boats was already stemming the tide to make for home, and Clem broke out *Miranda*'s anchor while George ran up her sails and headed them in her wake. In no hurry now, they stood at *Miranda*'s tiller and discussed the race, and Francis sat on the bundle of Melville's sails and watched George, still talking, put *Miranda* through the motley collection of boats that choked the river.

"We heard you were in a fight last night," George said to Matt. "It looks as if we heard right, too, by the look of you. It wouldn't have been anything to do with our friend, would it?"

Matt fingered his blood-caked jersey uneasily. "I don't know. It could have been," he muttered. He did not want to discuss the business, even with George.

"He won't love you any the more for the beating you gave him in public just now," George remarked gravely. "You'd best bide for a while, Matt, till he cools down. He's a dangerous man. I've said it before. Whoever attacked you last night, they reckoned to put you out of the way. I'll be surprised if Beckett didn't know something about it."

"It was a shock to him when I went aboard the yacht this morning," Matt recalled.

"Aye, and it was a shock to him when you went over the spit," George chuckled. "Did you see his face? It was as black as thunder."

Matt smiled, and even while he was smiling he knew that he had good cause to fear Beckett now. It wasn't a pretty thought. There were many ways a man might disappear round Marshfield, even without the help of a knife. And only George would guess at the truth, and he would have no proof at all. Matt stopped smiling and clasped his heavy, throbbing arm miserably, wishing now that the day was over and he was home in bed. He felt desperately tired now he had time to think about it, and his body ached in every limb. He had no wish to face Mr. Shelley again and no desire to explain away the missing drink to Henry. The water pageant and the fireworks could do without him. All he wanted was somebody's bunk.

As *Miranda* sailed up into Marchester she passed *Juno* on her mooring, deserted now, and slipped up under the stern of the *Good Fortune*. George sailed close and Francis and Matt jumped for it. Matt, using the last of his remaining strength, landed in a sprawling heap and would have slipped back into the water if Francis hadn't hauled him up by the scruff of his neck. He got dizzily to his feet and Francis propelled him gently to the forward companionway.

"You must sleep on board tonight," he said. "Beckett won't be using his bunk. Heaven knows what you did last night, but you look as if you could sleep for a week."

They stumbled down into the galley, where Henry was standing among a debris of chicken carcasses, empty tureens, stacked plates, and wine-dregs. A hubbub of conversation was coming from the saloon and a second steward was coming in, flushed and harassed, with another loaded tray. It was obvious that Mr. Shelley was celebrating his victory in no mean measure. Efficient and composed, Henry worked among the growing chaos in a cloud of steam and bubbling aromas, his face shining like a red apple, his fingers nimbling about the pots.

"Ah, Mr. Francis, sir, your father's waiting for you," he greeted them. "He went down to watch your smack race, and I hear you were on the winning boat. Congratulations, sir! Congratulations, Matt! I've kept your dinner by for you, sir."

"I hope there's some for Matt, too," Francis said, squeezing through to the saloon door. "I won't be a minute, Matt. I'll tell him we're back."

As he disappeared Henry looked up through the steam and said to Matt dryly, "I hear you did your celebrating somewhat prematurely. I shall know who not to send for the ale next time."

Matt was too weary to argue. "I'll pay you back when I get my wages," he said.

He leaned against the bulkhead, trying to keep his eyes open as the warmth from the stove enveloped him. It was only when Henry gave him a sudden nudge that he saw Mr. Shelley standing in the doorway of the galley. His face was shining through the steam like a red sun in the mist. Matt stumbled forward to face him and saw with a flood of relief that the face was all smiles, flushed and content with good food, good company, and the recollection of his victory.

"I saw you win your race," he said. "That was a splendid finish! There is no one I would sooner see take the prize, in spite of what happened last night. Can I believe your tale that it was none of your fault?"

"Yes, sir. I didn't get an arm like this of my own choosing."

Mr. Shelley looked at him meditatively. "You're a good

lad. There will always be a job for you on board this yacht when she's sailing."

He smiled and put a hand on Matt's shoulder. "Get Henry to fix you up now. He's as good a surgeon as he is a cook, so you've nothing to fear. Then you can have the captain's bunk for the night." He chuckled reminiscently, "You beat him fair and square, eh? We'll have to try you at the helm of the *Good Fortune* next and see what she does then."

Matt's heart gave a small leap at the last sentence; then he realized that Shelley was joking. He forced a smile, and Mr. Shelley disappeared back into the saloon. Henry stepped forward and steered Matt tenderly into the captain's quarters, where he sat him down on the bunk and stripped him of his jersy.

"I'll go up to The Barge myself next time," he muttered as he started to unwind the bloody mass of Matt's erstwhile best shirt, "if this is what you run into when you go for a bit of shopping."

If Henry had any suspicions, he kept them to himself. He proved himself as capable as Mr. Shelley had forecast, sewing up the wound with his chicken trussing needle and thread and finishing off as neatly as a seamstress. Francis, appearing at this delicate moment, felt the operation far more keenly than Matt, who had long ago learned stoicism in the face of pain and sat silent and unflinching until Henry had finished. Francis turned pale and set off briskly in search of yet another jersey for Matt, while Henry bandaged his work with a murmur of satisfaction.

"There, that's an improvement. I'm sure it feels better."

Matt nodded, wondering why Francis was bothering to find him clothes when all he wanted to do was roll over in

the bunk and fall asleep. Then the awful prospect dawned
on him: As winner of the smack race he would have to turn
out to receive his prize from the Mayor after the fireworks
display.

The rest of the evening passed Matt by in a dream. Without Francis's hand steady on his sound arm he would never
have found himself going through the right motions, reeling up through the bawling crowds, smiling grimly at the
glittering chain of office, shaking hands, receiving the
blessed little packet of sovereigns with a mumbled pleas-
antry. The sky, velvet-dark, was flowery with stars and the
lanterns shining up off the water. There were boats still
milling about everywhere and crowds dancing and singing
on the quays, crowds buffeting through the streets and running and rolling up the alleys. The fireworks lit the sky
with fountains of color, and the river below doubled and
reversed the patterns for good measure, so that Matt did not
know whether the stars in his head were real or imaginary,
whether he was awake or asleep. He had no recollection of
getting back to the yacht and tumbling into Beckett's bunk.
He only remembered the hard lump of the sovereigns under
his pillow, so hard and so real that they penetrated his ob-
livion, and he put up his hand and clasped them, and
slept.

When he awoke it was light, and quiet. He lay for a
while, taking in the soft, watery sunlight that filtered in
through the skylights and remembering, slowly, all the
things that had happened the day and night before. Then he
realized that he must see Melville, and he swung himself
painfully off the bunk, groping for his clothes. Henry was
in the galley, making tea, and he had a mug for Matt and
some hunks of bread and butter.

"Mr. Shelley's gone home. He left your pay for you," Henry said, handing over a packet.

"He's gone home? Has Francis gone, too?"

"Aye. He came in to see you, but he said he didn't want to wake you, and I'm to tell you he's coming over to Marshfield to fish with you in the winter."

Matt counted his money thoughtfully. "Is the *Good Fortune* now being laid up, then?" he asked.

"Aye. Mr. Shelley is going to Europe for three months. I believe Mr. Francis is going, too. But they've plans for sailing next summer. Beating *Juno* seems to have whetted Mr. Shelley's appetite for racing. He was talking of taking the yacht to Cowes next year."

Matt was surprised Francis had said nothing about going abroad, then remembered that traveling was something Francis took for granted. The regatta was over now, the race won, and Matt knew that his brief taste of yachting was finished for the summer. If Mr. Shelley was planning to go to Cowes, it might be finished for good, too. In spite of their kind words, Matt did not think he stood so high in the Shelleys' favor that they would seek him out to go with them when there were crews for the asking down there. He had a modest opinion of himself, and standing there in the galley, he suddenly knew that he was on his own again. The episode of the *Good Fortune* was over.

"How much do I owe you for the drink I lost?" he asked Henry.

"Mr. Shelley said I wasn't to take anything off you," Henry replied. "He made the money up to me himself."

Matt did not argue, but put the money away in his pocket. But for the episode of The Barge, Mr. Shelley would have been the poorer by a thousand pounds, so he felt justified in keeping his pay.

Henry wanted to say more to Matt, but the boy had a self-sufficiency that stopped him. Henry didn't think wounds like the one he had stopped were collected in festive brawls, and he hadn't been able to understand either why winning the race yesterday had put the skipper into such a bad humor. The landlord of the Plough and Sail would no doubt have a pithy opinion on the whole business, should he have an opportunity to speak with him. Henry looked at Matt curiously, and with compassion.

"Are you going ashore, then?" he asked. "I'll row you off."

Matt followed the steward down into the skiff and sat in silence as Henry pulled over to Melville's yard. The boat-builder was in his office and smiled broadly when he saw Matt.

"You did it, then?" he said, shaking Matt enthusiastically by the hand. "Your old *Fathom* won the race! That was a fine bit of sailing, even if you did break the old girl up. I suppose you've come to ask me when the new one will be ready."

"Yes, I have. I shall be wanting her badly."

"Well, we'll get on with her as fast as we can. I reckon we can have her ready for the middle of September if that will suit you."

"The middle of September? As long as that?"

"There's the sails to be made yet, lad, and you can see for yourself she's barely got her decks on. I don't see my way to finishing her any sooner, not so that you've still got a good boat."

Matt nodded. The prospect of six weeks without a boat to work was frightening, but he knew Melville was right when he said she could not be ready any sooner.

"I've got my prize money here," he said. "I meant it for you, but I'll have to keep some of it to feed us the next month. Here, we'll halve it."

"I'm in no hurry for it, lad, if your family's in need."

"But I'm in a hurry for you to have it," Matt said. "It's all I shall think about, until the smack is paid for. There's still plenty owing, even with this."

Melville pocketed his share reluctantly. "Don't worry, boy," he said. "We'll have your boat ready for the spratting. Then you'll start making some money."

"I only hope so," Matt replied. "Did George bring your sails back last night?"

"Aye, he did."

"Well, my business is done here. I might as well start for home. It looks as if I shall have to walk it, too."

The visiting smacks had all gone out on the morning tide, *Miranda* with them, but Matt, without a boat, had nothing to hurry for. He was going to miss plenty more tides before *Reward* was ready for him. As he walked up along the quays towards the bridge he felt very much on his own again. He had not realized before how much he had been fortified by the promise of work, and even friendship, from the influential Shelley family. It was only now, when that was gone, that he saw how hard the immediate future—the coming winter—promised to be. He would have forty pounds to find for Melville still, and only old Aaron to help him; and if the season was bad, he knew he would be lucky to feed the family, let alone save towards his debt. The loss of *Fathom* and the pain in his arm made him feel sick and pessimistic. The dusty lane was not his province anyway, and as the sun grew hotter he wished more and more that he had woken earlier and caught *Miranda* before she sailed.

With a sea breeze to cool his sweat he would not be feeling so wretched. Across the fields, tawny with ripening corn, the sea was as smooth as a silk ribbon, the mud flats shimmering with the rising heat. But Matt saw no beauty. He was conscious only of forebodings and fears as he trudged on. When eventually, helped on his way by a lift in a farm cart, he walked down the track to his own cottage, he felt as if he had been away for weeks.

Beckett stayed late in the Plough and Sail, drinking heavily in a shadowed corner away from the bar. He was alone, and the rest of the smacksmen were content to leave him so. It was not difficult for Beckett to sense their satisfaction with the outcome of the Marchester regatta; the laughing and chatting emphasized his own isolation. He was used to being alone among his fellow smacksmen, but by virtue of his power, not humiliation. He had come to believe that his cunning was sufficient to see him master of any situation, and his arrogance had suffered a crashing blow. He fidgeted with his glass, glowering into the smoky light. His heavy features were not improved by a cut and swollen lip and bruises about the eyes; his friends, having lost more than a thousand pounds between them, had not been content with verbal abuse. Yet Beckett's rancor was not concerned with them. It was concerned wholly with Matt Pullen. Confident for so long in his own strength, he could perhaps have accepted defeat by superior forces, a boatload of excise men, or even by a man as influential as Peregrine Shelley, but to be brought low by a lad as unexceptional as Matt Pullen was beyond Beckett's comprehension. The vision of Matt's bloody, stubborn face across the *Good Fortune*'s helm haunted Beckett with a persistence that maddened him. Even his drinking did not drown the memory.

"Mr. Beckett."

He looked up suspiciously to see George Firmin standing in front of him.

"Well?"

"I want a word with you." Without waiting for an invitation George pulled out a chair and sat down. His voice was low and steady. "I don't know how Matt Pullen got that knife wound in his arm, for he's not telling anyone, but one thing I do know. If anything happens to Matt, I'll see you swing for it."

Beckett's eyes gleamed. "What's that to me? What happens to Matt Pullen is his own business."

"You didn't get where you are by respecting anyone that crossed your path. I know your sort. You've only one answer for anyone weaker than yourself. And it's not a pretty one. You reckon Matt could be found drowned, perhaps, and no one'd know it wasn't an accident. You're too clever to use a knife a second time—I'm not underestimating you. But I just want to warn you, that's all. If anything happens to Matt, I'll make sure you get hanged for it."

Beckett said nothing. George, who had been half afraid that he would get his teeth knocked down his throat for his trouble, did not linger to soften his words with any less urgent conversation. He stood up and went out of the inn into the warm summer darkness. He was relieved that he had found the courage to give Beckett his warning, but the expression in Beckett's eyes had given him no comfort.

"Please God I'm wrong in what I'm thinking," he said to himself as he walked down the hill to his home.

The *Rose in June*

The next six weeks of summer were the longest Matt had
ever known.

"For goodness' sake, stop fretting and take a holiday," his
mother told him. "It will be the first of your life—and your
last, most likely, so make the best of it."

But Matt found no pleasure in wandering over the sea
walls and idling on the little shell beaches of the estuary
when he could see the sails of the fleet working out along
the edge of the Buxey sand. He would lie there on the
springy dried roots of the sea lavender watching the midget
specks of canvas on the water and longing to be one of them.
Time on his hands was only time for thinking, and his
thoughts turned always to the same subject: Would he
prove, this coming winter, that he could provide for the
family and still find the money to repay Melville? Aaron
seemed to be growing older and slower week by week; the
twins never looked like growing more responsible. They
would be twelve by Christmas, and Matt knew that he
would be able to persuade his mother to let him have them
on the smack when the spring came, but equally well he
knew nothing would persuade her to consent to their sailing
sooner. As he lay moodily watching the scuttling antics of a

crab on the mud, he told himself he should be grateful for the luck that had given him the piloting of the schooner and the introduction to Mr. Shelley, but somehow the incidents of the summer meant little to him now. If he had thought that he had any future with the *Good Fortune*, it might have been different, but since he had learned that she was going to Cowes, he felt that the sooner he forgot all about her the better. Fishing was his future, and if he wanted any comfort, he had better think of his new smack rather than the glossy delights of Mr. Shelley's racing yacht.

He turned over on his back and watched the high white clouds making pictures over the sea. He was almost seventeen now, and had the shoulders and arms on him of a man. His brown face was bonier and fine-drawn, the once candid blue eyes more cautious and watchful, but his impetuous, restless movements were still those of a boy. It was a boy's nature that set him to skimming flat stones across the water to see how far they would hop and, eventually, sent him jumping over the channels in the saltings to see how good a steeplechaser he was. If he had had his own way, he would have been crewing on someone else's smack out there these past few weeks, but his mother had enlisted the doctor's help in persuading him otherwise, for the wound in his arm had been bad enough to have killed a weaker specimen after the way it had been treated the day of the regatta. But now, thanks to his good counsel, Matt had only a purple scar to remind him of Beckett's treachery.

Of Beckett himself he dared not think at all. There was enough to frighten him in the thought of supporting his family, without letting his mind dwell on Beckett's intentions. Matt did not fool himself into believing that Beckett had finished with him. He knew Beckett was waiting his chance. It might come in a week, or a year, or five years.

There was no way of knowing. It might never come. But Matt was withdrawn and watchful and nervous in a way his mother could not understand, and it was because of Beckett, not the fishing.

At the end of Matt's fifth week of idleness a message came by carrier from Marchester to say that the *Reward* was on the water and would be ready to sail away in a few days' time. Three days later Matt begged a lift in a farm cart to Marchester and made his way to Melville's yard, where he saw *Reward* afloat for the first time, riding to her anchor where the *Good Fortune* had lain and, to Matt's eyes, no less beautiful than the yacht. As he looked at her, Matt knew that she would decide his fate one way or the other. She would give him no excuse for failure. He went to see Melville, and presently the yard manager was rowing him out to go on board. This was the moment Matt had waited for, and now it had arrived he went about getting up sail in a dream. He could not get out of his head the thought of his father. He felt that his father was with him, chuckling with excitement and shouting out his orders. And when he was sailing the feeling persisted. Matt almost found himself pointing out the remains of *Fathom* to this obtrusive ghost. It was with mixed feelings that he brought the new boat into her home creek for the first time, and threw out her anchor in the wake of the moored fleet.

Although it was almost dark, his mother and the twins were on the sea wall waiting for him, and George Firmin came out in his skiff to fetch him off.

"She's fine, Matt. You'll do all right with her," George said.

The twins were capering as usual, and clamoring to have a look aboard, but Matt was tired and felt sad rather than elated. He knew his mother shared his feelings, for as they went towards the hard, she looked back at the new smack and said, "How your father would have loved to see her lying here!"

Now Matt went back to the familiar routine, going out on the tide, dropping the anchor in a likely spot, and streaming the stow net for sprats. With only two of them to handle it the full net was hard work, and it was impossible for two hands to get as much on board during a day's fishing as the four Beckett brothers or the three Firmins. And Matt knew that Aaron was failing. His strength was no more than a child's. When they sailed home on the making tide *Charity* and *Miranda* would often be sailing with decks almost awash, sluggish with the weight of their catch, but *Reward* never knew how it felt to have more than half her hold full. Matt would stand at the tiller, wracked with weariness, and go past the laden smacks with a feeling of despair. In two months he saved only three pounds toward his debt to Melville and even for that he knew his mother had gone short. When his mother served sprats for supper and Joe sat down at the table with a grimace, Matt would have hit him if Mary Pullen hadn't pulled him back in time.

"All right, let him come and catch them, then he won't turn his nose up at them!" Matt shouted.

"He'll eat sprats for every meal rather than go on that smack before he's twelve," his mother retorted sharply. "What do you want for a crew, a pair of babies?"

Later, when the twins were in bed, she said, "The spring is soon enough, Matt. We can manage this winter, the way we're going now."

Matt, less sure, held his peace. He knew his mother was right, that it was no way to introduce the boys to fishing by starting them in November. But as he went aboard next day and headed *Reward* out into a short sullen sea he wondered what was the use of this new ship without a crew to sail her? Aaron seemed to grow more frail day by day. It was as if the spirit had gone out of him since Tom Pullen was drowned, and the idleness of the summer weeks seemed to have brought on a final apathy that he made no effort to throw off. He went through the motions on board, but Matt found himself obliged to take charge of more and more until it seemed to him that he was virtually working single-handed. He knew then that those grinding weeks that followed his father's death, before he met distraction in the shape of the *Good Fortune*, were to be repeated, that they were the pattern for his future. To earn a living, let alone repay his debt, he must work every hour he could keep his eyes open.

November brought frost and days of stinging rain and sleet. Handling the nets on a pitching sleet-wet deck became the be-all and end-all of Matt's existence. *Reward* was an easier boat to work than *Fathom*, for she was lower to the water and had a flat counter stern instead of the old-fashioned transom, but she was wetter and less comfortable into the bargain. Matt came to distinguish each day only by its more or less degrees of discomfort. There was no relief in the hours he spent on deck, save in the form of an hour of sunlight, or a friendly shout from the passing *Miranda*, and no relief from the incessant demands of the trawl and the gear, and the sullenness of the winter sea. When he was home he ate and slept and then crawled out of bed to start the round again, stumbling down to the sea wall with a lantern in his hand. The sprats were at their best and none of the smacks were wasting time in idleness. The fleet seemed always to be coming or going, the creek stinking of the perpetual stream of fish and the sweat of the cart horses that struggled through the mud.

One night when he had landed his catch Matt went up to his cottage with a feeling of worse depression than usual, for Aaron had crushed his hand in the fairlead and by the look of it he would be of less use than ever for the next week or so. It was raining and a bitter northeasterly had done its best to keep the fleet from getting home at all, and after eighteen hours away Matt had no thought beyond his meal and the welcome warmth of the fire. Pushing open the kitchen door, he stood dripping and blinking in the lamp-light, shaking his wet hair up off his forehead.

"Matt, you've got a visitor," his mother said as she came to meet him.

Her voice was slightly anxious, and for one moment Matt thought he was going to have to face his Uncle Albert again. Then, glancing across the kitchen, he saw Francis standing in front of the fire.

"Francis!"

In that moment he didn't know whether he loved or hated Francis. He had not thought of him for weeks, and his last feelings towards him had been of a rather bitter indulgence, based on envy. Francis could afford to sail for pleasure. His desire to come fishing, Matt had decided, was a whim to amuse himself by seeing how his baser fellows lived. But now he was with him again, face to face, Matt was not so sure. There was no patronization in Francis's look, only a respectful sort of affection that disarmed Matt. He felt his heart lift and he smiled slowly.

"What are you doing here?"

"I'm hoping you'll sign me on as crew," Francis said. "The lowest order, of course. I'll work for my keep, if you'll have me."

"Do you really want to come?" Matt asked doubtfully, crossing over to the fire. As he stripped off his clothes, sodden to the skin, he realized that at least Francis could see now that fishing in November wasn't quite the same as the shrimping they had enjoyed in June. He was cold and exhausted, and Francis, no doubt, had eyes in his head to remark the fact.

"I thought you were never getting back," Mary Pullen said, handing him a towel from the fire. "Mr.—er—Francis has been here since it went dark. I was beginning to think you'd be out another tide."

"The wind's offshore," Matt said. "And the tide turned just as we were in the creek mouth. Aaron's cracked his hand—if you're serious about crewing, Francis, you've chosen the right moment."

He toweled himself down, shrugged into a dry shirt and trousers, and sat at the table to devour his dinner.

"What does your father say to your coming?" he asked between mouthfuls.

"He didn't stop me," Francis said briefly.

"You're welcome here, anyway," Matt said abruptly. Thawed by the warmth of the kitchen and the dinner in his stomach, he was remembering Francis's kindness the night of the regatta, Francis handling the sheets when old *Fathom* shot her bolt over Butler's spit. He looked up and grinned at him, glad now—more than he could have expressed—to see Francis again. "I'm glad you've come," he said.

When Francis had come home after three months' grinding study in Paris, his first idea had been to find Matt and go sailing with him. The fact that it was winter made no difference to him.

"You're mad," his father said shortly.

"Father, I'm not asking much," Francis said stubbornly. (Three months ago, his father noted, he would never have spoken to him so forthrightly.) "This will be my last chance to sail and work with Matt. Once I'm at Oxford it will all be different. You know how I feel about the smacks! I can learn more from Matt in a week than in a season of being a passenger on *Good Fortune*. I'm sick of books and studies! A few weeks at Marshfield, and I promise you I'll be satisfied."

It was the shrewd Henry who decided Mr. Shelley to give Francis his head. "It will cure him once and for all, fishing at this time of the year," he remarked when his employer went so far as to ask him for his opinion.

"Kill him more likely," Mr. Shelley snapped. But he had to admit that the boy had perhaps been hard pressed with his books; it was natural that the simple, physical life at Marshfield would appeal.

Francis had packed and left at once. He was not expecting it to be easy this time and, for his part, Matt did not dare to ask him how long he intended to stay. He was sure in his own mind that two or three days would be enough to convince him that there were better places to be than on a smack on the fringe of the North Sea in November. But although Francis was often green with seasickness as *Reward* pitched out to her fishing grounds and his hands burned with sores and he was often so tired that he felt he was working in a dream (or a nightmare), the days passed and Francis made no reference to leaving. Matt, afraid to spoil his luck, held his tongue. The two of them worked together, ate together, and slept in the same room under the sagging roof. Henry visited the Plough and Sail and made discreet inquiries from time to time, but Francis bore him no resentment. The Pullen family quickly lapsed into treating Francis as one of themselves, and Matt found that, although the work was still hard and the weather bitter, the worst of the hardship seemed to dissolve in this sharing of responsibility. The strain went from Matt's face and he laughed with Francis over the supper table. Hearing him, Mary Pullen thought she felt a few of her own wrinkles easing.

Two weeks before Christmas *Reward* was caught in a sudden gale off the south edge of the Buxey sand. Matt, having struck a good haul, wanted to get as much aboard as he could. Comforted by the fact that with the wind in the northwest he was in a relatively safe position on a weather shore (if "shore" it could properly be termed, Francis thought to himself as he looked across at a line of white breakers marking the shoal—there was no actual land in sight at all), he went on streaming the stow net until the last moment. By the time he had decided to call it a day and was at the jib halyards hauling in the net the sky was darkening fast. *Reward* was snubbing restlessly on her anchor. The sprats streamed into the hold, a glittering flood in the last struggling glimmer of twilight over the horizon. Darkness and gale came together, flinging down a deluge of cold rain as the two boys secured the net on the deck.

"We're safe enough here till it eases," Matt shouted into the wind. "I'll let some more chain out. Go below!"

Francis was only too thankful to obey as he clawed his way along the pitching deck. For all his determination, he knew he was a long way from achieving Matt's magnificent indifference to physical discomfort. He had yet to see Matt flinch or hesitate in conditions that Francis could only think of as sheer hell.

So much for my thinking I could be a smacksman, he thought as he sat shivering in the darkness of *Reward*'s cuddy forward. Qualms of sickness in an empty stomach did little to reassure him.

Matt came down, shedding a heap of soaked outer clothing. He lit a paraffin lamp and soon got a wood fire going in the stove.

"At least we've a bunk each with Aaron crocked up," he said as he fed the fire. Aaron's crushed hand had festered, and Matt had told him to stay at home till it mended. "Not that they're up to the *Good Fortune*'s standard, I'm afraid," he added with a faint smile at the memory of the last time he had sat with Francis before a saloon fire. He liked to see the new smack's cuddy lit by the lamp and the fire, the timbers still pale and new, the floor dry as a bone. "We'd be pumping now, if this was old *Fathom*."

He filled a kettle from the water cask and hung it over the stove on a hook, where it swayed wildly, to increase Francis's feeling of nausea. Matt, noticing the drawn, greenish cheeks, nodded towards the straw mattress and said, "Get your head down. You can sleep it out. Look, there's a dry jersey in the locker."

He pulled it out, the old *Good Fortune* jersey with the knife slit in the sleeve neatly darned and the faint, not-quite-washed-out bloodstains. As he exchanged it gratefully for his soaked shirt, Francis, distracted from his sickness, said, "Did you really get that arm in a roughhouse?"

It was the first time the subject had been mentioned since they had met again. Matt hesitated. In that moment he knew that he would dearly love to spill out the tale of Beckett's treachery to Francis. Equally well, he knew he could not. There would come a time for it, he thought, but it wasn't now.

"Yes," he said. As the wind howled in the rigging outside he added, "There will be some ships in trouble tonight, I reckon."

Francis, comforted by the fact that Matt obviously didn't include *Reward* among the number, fell into an uneasy sleep. He knew Matt was lying about his arm. A few fragments of the conversation which he had overheard on board *Miranda* after the smack race had suggested that Beckett was responsible, but the fact that Matt did not wish to implicate Beckett, even to him, only increased Francis's regard for him. Several times through the night he heard Matt go up on deck and check that the anchor wasn't dragging. The wind eased and in the small hours, with the tide flooding, Matt got the smack under way again. The wind had gone round northerly, and if it stayed that way, he thought he would be home by dawn. The rest of the fleet had gone home the afternoon before and he knew his mother would be worried. The gale had blown itself out, leaving a lumpy sea and lead-black sky. Matt picked up the Spitway buoy, put the smack about and stood hunched at the tiller, his eyes half-shut against the bitter wind. But at least his hold was fuller than it had ever been. He had no regrets on that score.

Although it was dark, there was a moon somewhere behind the ragged cloud. Matt, glancing towards the line of sullen breakers that marked the edge of the Gunfleet, thought he saw the hulk of a boat in the darkness. It certainly had no lights, and whether it was there at all he couldn't help doubting as his eyes kept returning to the line of the breakers. If it existed, it must be a wreck, and Matt's heart started to race at the possibility. He knew he could not sail on home without investigating, so, once clear of the shoal, he put *Reward* about again and started sailing close-hauled to where the darker shadow in an all-pervading darkness tantalized his eyes.

"Are we on our way home?"

Francis put his head sleepily out of the hatch, shuddering as the wind caught his warm face.

"You should have woken me," he added, guiltily.

"Can you see anything over there on the starboard bow?" Matt demanded urgently.

Francis stared bleakly into the night. "There's a dark shape. Is that what you mean? A boat?"

"It is there, then! I was half thinking my eyes were playing tricks!" Matt exclaimed eagerly. "I told you there would be boats in trouble last night!"

His blood was racing with anticipation as *Reward* pitched on over the foul tide. He felt no compunction for his excitement either. He had hardened since his father's death.

As *Reward* slowly bit her way through the choppy shoal water, the dark shadow revealed itself as a big smack of about twenty tons. Matt shouted as they sailed by her, but there was no response. The forlorn shadow, swept by the ribbons of her sails, tossed dejectedly on the edge of the sand, held there by the flood and the last efforts of the gale that had wrecked her.

"We'll have a look at her," Matt said excitedly, bringing *Reward* up into the wind. "Let go the anchor!" he shouted to Francis as he loosed the halyards and quickly dropped the stiff wet mass of the mainsail and foresails to the deck. The next moment they were in the skiff and pulling rapidly for the wreck.

"Can you see her name?"

Matt ran the boat under her stern and Francis was able to peer at the once-gilded letters.

"*Rose* something," Francis murmured. "*Rose in June*, I think it is."

Matt was already aboard, the skiff painter in his hand.

"She's not from round here, then."

Her sails were blown to shreds and she was making water, although not too rapidly as far as they could judge. It was over the floorboards in the cuddy. Matt waded in and lit the candles he had brought with him, illuminating the usual bare and unwelcoming pit with its cramped bunks and rusty stove. Already his mind was working on a plan of campaign.

"She's too heavy to tow along," he said, half to himself.

Francis was as yet unaware of the rules of salvage. He followed the thoughtful Matt back to the deck and watched him drop the anchor over the bows. The smack wallowed heavily, the lumpy seas occasionally washing her deck. Matt tried the pump and found to his satisfaction that it worked.

"Francis, do you think you could sail *Reward* home, alone, and get the Firmin brothers to come out here?"

He faced Francis gravely in the darkness, his hands still on the pump handle. Even in the gloom he was able to make out the flash of alarm in Francis's eyes. But the voice that replied was steady enough.

"I could try."

"I wish to God we had Aaron with us," Matt muttered. Then, forgetting the possibility in the same instant: "One of us must stay aboard here to lay claim to her. But by dawn you could have the Firmins on their way. I cannot leave *you*, for she's like enough to sink before long if our luck goes against us, and I'd sooner drown myself than face your father if you got drowned. What do you say to it? I don't think you'll have any trouble."

Francis nodded. "I'll do my best."

"I'll get *Reward* sailing for you. You'll have the flood under you. Come on! The sooner you get going the better!"

Matt's words tumbled out in his eagerness to carry through

his plan. The fact that Francis had accepted the idea that
he could sail *Reward* home, without any arguing or words
of doubt, warmed him with admiration for his aristocratic
deck hand. He rowed strongly back to *Reward* and set about
hauling up the mainsail. The smack was lying on a lee
shore, and to get her off without putting her aground required a certain amount of skill. Matt guessed that Francis
could have done it, but the prize at stake was too big to
risk delay. They went forward and got the anchor straight
up and down and set the big staysail, then when Francis
broke out the anchor Matt backed the staysail and *Reward*
paid off obediently, clear of danger. Matt went back to the
helm, put her about and pointed her bowsprit in the direction of Marshfield.

"Keep this course and you should be in the creek by the
time it gets light. Tell George to bring a spare mains'l."
As the smack slipped past the dark shape of the *Rose in
June*, Matt handed over the tiller and loosed the skiff
painter. In a moment he had pulled the boat close and
stepped in, and from the darkness Francis heard his voice,
"Good luck!"

Then Francis knew he was on his own.

It rained before the light came, a stinging drizzle misting
the black shape of the mainsail. Francis's face ached with
the cold, and his feet, cramped in old Tom Pullen's sea
boots, might have been left aboard the wreck for all he
could feel of them. But Francis, for once, had as little regard for his human condition as the admired Matt, for it
was excitement and pride, not cold, that made his fingers
tremble on the tiller. Having put his trust in Matt's course,
he had held the surging smack straight and true to carve an
uncompromising wake through the night, at the same time

thanking providence with all his heart that the wind had remained on the beam and he had not had to tack. One turn about in the thick dark, and not all his mathematics, he felt, would have seen him right thereafter. Matt, he felt sure, did not do it by mathematics, but Francis knew—now more than ever—that smacksmen's instincts were not acquired overnight.

The late, miserable dawn showed him to his infinite satisfaction that he was right off the Marshfield creek. He thought he could see a sail coming out, but it was too far away to hail. He put the smack about for the first time and headed her for home. The tide was almost high and he had the full width of the creek in which to make his big clumsy boards. *Reward* hesitated for him, where for Matt she would shoot away on the opposite tack like a wheeling bird, but the tide kept pushing her home, even as she sulked under his inexperience. Francis fidgeted with impatience. As the cold light spread he could see a gaff over the sea wall, moving slowly against the flood, and he guessed that the smacks were making use of the fair wind to make an early start. As he reached the dog's-leg bend a long bowsprit slipped out from behind the wall, and Francis recognized *Miranda*'s number on the bow. He bawled out George's name, and in his excitement got *Reward* in irons again, so that she fell back, her mainsail flogging angrily, her rudder churning up soft mud.

But George had heard his frantic hail. In a moment *Miranda* was sliding past his bows, and George jumped aboard.

"Where's Matt?"

Francis was surprised at the sharp fear in his voice.

"He's all right. We found a wreck and he stayed aboard and sent me to fetch you."

George put the tiller over with a massive, firm hand and *Reward* stopped her antics instantly and glided off the mud. George's whole attention was on Francis, his honest blue eyes looking at him with a whole mixture of emotions. Fear was still uppermost, the boy noticed.

"What's this wreck? What state is she in?" he asked.

"It's a big smack on the Gunfleet. She's no sail on, and is fairly full of water, but Matt seemed to think you could get her home between you. Her pump is working."

"On the Gunfleet," George murmured. "Who is she, d'you know?"

"The *Rose in June*," Francis replied.

If the name had meant nothing to Matt, Francis thought, it seemed to mean a lot more to George. A startled expression crossed his face. Already he was trimming the mainsheet, and *Reward* was heading fast back the way she had come. *Miranda* was just ahead, the two Firmin brothers looking back curiously.

"My God, the *Rose in June!*" George muttered. He looked sharply at Francis. "Did you see a sail go out of the creek ahead of you? You must have done, lad!" Without waiting for a reply he went on, "That was Beckett, heading for the Gunfleet. And Matt alone on the *Rose in June!*"

Now there was no doubt about the fear in George's eyes. Francis's warm feelings of achievement died away and he stood coldly as the fear took root in his own mind.

"Beckett?" he repeated. He remembered the darn in the white jersey, and Matt's stubborn lie.

"This is the chance Beckett has been waiting for," George said. "He will kill Matt this time."

Beckett

Matt, alone on the groaning, rolling deck of the abandoned smack, put out of his mind the example of Aaron, whose lunacy had been caused by being left alone on an abandoned wreck for two days and nights, and dwelt instead on the thought of the prize money he stood to gain from this night's work. He worked at the pump patiently, but saw little result for his labor. The smack still rode low, slightly down by the bows, but not low enough yet to worry him unduly. She snubbed restlessly to her anchor, and her old timbers complained, strained and crippled by the hours of pounding on the hard sand. Matt guessed there were plenty of leaks below her water line, but there was little he could do now to set about making repairs. The noise, constant as the breaking of the surf on the receding sand, was almost a comfort to him in his cold vigil, as if the old smack was grumbling aloud about her undeserved treatment. In fact, Matt found himself talking back.

Why did they leave you, old girl? he wondered as he labored on the pump. You aren't so far gone.

But at the height of the gale it would have felt different, he supposed. Since the times of the Romans the Gunfleet must have had a wreck to every square yard of her gleaming ebb-tide spread. God knows the bones and spars that went to make up her grains of sand, Matt thought.

"Very likely you're only worth a load of sprats yourself," he muttered. "But just pay my debt to Melville and I shan't worry." A drizzling rain started to come in on the wind and Matt went below and lit the candles again. The water was higher in the cuddy, but not alarmingly so; he could still sit on the bunk without getting his trousers wet. He thought of Francis sailing *Reward* home, and smiled at the memory of his last glimpse of the set white face glancing back over the stern. But he wasn't worried about Francis. His eyes roved round the dismal cuddy, which was showing the results of the hull's pounding. The forward bulkhead had split, and some wooden crates had slid out. Something glinted in the candlelight. Idly Matt stepped across to investigate.

Even before his hand closed on the crate he realized what he had found, and why the crew of the *Rose in June* had been so loath to stay with their boat. No, and if he'd been the skipper, he thought, as his eyes roamed over the contents of the forepeak, he'd have made off in a cockleshell of a rowing boat in a gale of wind rather than be found in charge of six dozen bottles of French brandy. The glass winked through its rough straw packing.

"Aye, you old rogue!" Matt breathed to the old smack. "So that's what you're about! I wonder where you were making for last night. Up one of the creeks, I'll be bound, and no one'd be the wiser by dawn. Perhaps you'll be worth my trouble, after all!"

Merely looking at the brandy warmed Matt's heart. He did not need to sample it to feel the blood coursing through his veins with excitement. This was a haul worth more than the groaning old boat herself—and what if he hadn't bothered to stop and investigate a shadow on the Gunfleet, when the wind had been going through his ribs like a knife and home had beckoned so strongly! The find put new life into Matt. Blowing out the candles he hurried back on deck and started work at the pump again, swearing to keep at it till dawn, when he hoped he would see *Miranda*'s patched sail against the first light. He hadn't worked on a pump since *Fathom* had sailed her last. It was a pleasant thought. His big calloused hands shoved the handle remorselessly backwards and forwards, and the dirty stream from her bilges laced the sea astern. Veils of misty rain cooled Matt's sweat. But he was happy.

Imperceptibly, the darkness paled. By full flood the sky was light over Marshfield, and Matt thought he saw the dark patch of a sail coming in his direction. The Gunfleet now was an innocent expanse of choppy sea, metal-gray under the sour December dawn.

"You dirty old wrecker," Matt muttered to its hidden breast, as the pump went on spraying out the same water that—Matt had no doubt—was seeping in as fast somewhere between those torn timbers below.

"Come on, George," he said and, with a grin to himself, "I'll be able to offer 'em drinks all round. Just like Mr. Shelley."

By now the patch that Matt had thought was a sail had revealed itself as a smack heading in his direction. If it was George, Matt wondered why *Reward* wasn't with him, too. If it wasn't George . . . Matt straightened up and stared keenly across the water. If it wasn't George, it wouldn't matter. Anyone else would acknowledge his claim to the *Rose in June*. Only if it were . . .

"My God," said Matt softly.

Of all the contingencies that might arise, this was one that had quite eluded him. Matt's hands dropped to his sides and clenched despairingly. Beckett! And he alone on a wreck, with fathoms of drowning water under him and no one to know that he had not slipped and fallen, no one to see Beckett's hands round his windpipe! And no doubt, Matt thought bitterly as his fate came vividly into his mind's eye, Beckett would know the secret of the *Rose in June* before he even set eyes on the forepeak, for Beckett knew everything that was a secret from the revenue men at Marchester.

"That's *Charity* all right," Matt murmured. She was moving as fast as a revenue cutter herself. Matt stared at her with a sick fear settling like lead in his stomach. In spite of the sweat on his face he felt himself shivering and he knew he was afraid, as afraid as he had been in The Barge at Marchester, and with as good reason.

I beat Beckett then, he thought wildly. I can do it again. But for the life of him he could not see how. There was no escape. He stood stock-still, watching the white bow wave lifting under *Charity*'s stem as she ran down towards the wreck, and he stopped trembling and lifted his chin.

"All right, Mr. Beckett," he said softly. "Just you come. We'll finish it one way or another."

He had a marlinespike hanging from his belt, his only weapon.

Charity wore round and went past an arm's length away. One of Beckett's brothers was at the tiller, and Beckett stood with the other on the deck with his fists on his thighs. He saw the name of the smack across her transom and said something to his brothers and laughed. Of Matt he took no notice at all.

"You keep clear, Mr. Beckett!" Matt shouted. "George Firmin is coming to help me with this. She's mine!"

Even to himself his voice sounded as unimpressive as the

squawking of a hungry gull, chasing *Charity*'s wake. As he anticipated, the smack reached past well beyond the *Rose in June,* then went about and came back, bearing down on her. Beckett stepped forward and stood ready to jump, one hand on the shrouds. Matt knew there was no chance of an accident. *Charity*'s jib came sliding past. The two bulwarks had mere inches between them as Beckett stepped across. For all his huge body he moved as neatly as a dancer, and without a pause came across the deck to where Matt still stood by the pump.

Even then all he said was, "You're not much of a swimmer, eh, Matt Pullen? Let's see what you can do." And the big fists came up from his thighs and thrust at Matt's shoulders to tip him off balance. But as Matt saw them move he ducked and darted under the outstretched arm. Beckett spun around, but Matt, in two strides, was at the shrouds and grasping up for the ratlines.

"Ah, you brat!" Beckett muttered.

He lunged after him, but his hand caught only a sharp kick from Matt's boot as the boy put his trust in the frayed rope and scrambled up the haven of the mast. It was an instinctive move, and Matt had no time to consider its advantages or otherwise as he clawed his way up. Beckett cursed at the shrouds, looking after him, then with an oath he swung his heavy body up in pursuit. His big arms stretched up like a gorilla's and Matt, watching him sharply, saw the folds of his heavy jersey lift to reveal a money belt at his waist. Whose money belt it was Matt had not an instant doubt, for the heavy gilt buckle was immediately familiar to him. It was the same belt which, in the days before his father had had any money to cumber it with, had whistled painfully round his own anatomy on occasion, the same belt that, full of the *Seaflower* sovereigns, had dragged

his father to his death. Matt knew he wasn't likely to mistake it, even though round Beckett's girth it was extended to its last hole. Matt even glimpsed the worn mark where his father had notched it round his own skinny stomach. In that moment, Matt's fear left him.

"You won't get me under those waves, Mr. Beckett, not unless I take you with me!" he muttered under his breath.

Beckett crawled up the ratlines, swearing as the frayed rope gave way once or twice beneath his weight. Matt, clinging like a monkey to the top of the mast, swung in nauseating circles as the old wreck rolled on the slack tide, wind-rode to her anchor. Far away he could see the sails of *Miranda* and *Reward*, but they were too far away to be of any use to him now. Matt got a firm handhold on the block swinging at his shoulder and thanked God that he still had his boots on. As Beckett's black head came up below him he drew back one leg and kicked out.

But Beckett was no fool. Quick as light his great fist flashed up and grasped Matt's ankle. He yanked viciously, but Matt's arms were as strong as his own. Matt knew the grip he had on the block meant the difference between life and death, and he heard his sockets crack as Beckett pulled again. With a gasp, he unwrapped his other leg from the mast, and hanging by his arms, he made a second despairing kick at Beckett's temple. As he kicked, the smack rolled and he felt himself thrown outwards, dangling over space. Beckett lost his balance, the roll and Matt's boot together throwing him heavily backwards, and as he fell he screamed, more in rage than in pain. Simultaneously, as if in the knowledge that he had won, Matt's wracked hands lost their grip and the two of them fell together.

Matt saw the flash of the water below him. Beckett, hanging outwards from the ratlines at the moment Matt's boot caught him, plunged spreadeagled and screaming into the sea, but Matt, dropping from the mast itself, hit the shrouds and was checked in his fall. He bounced off, burning a frantic hand on the rope stay, and landed in a crumpled heap on the deck.

Charity, swooping to her skipper's aid, saw the eddy on the water where he had gone under. The two brothers jibed the smack, panic-stricken to reach it, but the wind had already blown the bubbles away and no black head reappeared. Dimly Matt heard the brothers shouting and running along *Charity*'s deck, as he had shouted and run across *Fathom*'s deck when his father had drowned, and he thought of the money belt at Beckett's waist, holding him down with its good solid weight, just as it had done for his father.

Maybe your brothers will trawl for *you*, Matt thought

with a fine sense of retribution, and through the dizzying haze before his eyes he saw *Reward* and *Miranda*, hurrying like police cutters out of the grayness of the morning. *Charity* went about once more and sheered off, and Matt dragged himself to his feet and stood shakily grasping the shrouds. Strangely, at the climax of his year-long fight with Beckett, he felt nothing now, no horror, no triumph, no surprise, only an overwhelming feeling of weariness.

Reward looked very good as she came alongside the wreck's lee.

The village of Marshfield was humming with the news of the incident on the Gunfleet long before the *Rose in June* eventually limped home on the flood

late in the evening. Half the village seemed to be down at the creek, weaving respectfully about the dark-uniformed figures of a group of police and Excise men from Marchester. Matt was reminded grimly of carnival night in Marchester. He felt much the same, too, as he had then, half stupid with weariness, while he helped warp the floundering *Rose in June* upon the mud and answered questions and watched the illicit cargo of his precious salvage noted and docketed and unloaded into a couple of the willing, excited skiffs that swilled about the cold flood. The rest of the fleet was unloading at the same time (the customs official in charge of the brandy was careful to keep an unblinking eye on his responsibilities as he supervised its journey ashore), and the hard echoed with the bawling of the unloading smacksmen, the swearing of the carters, and the excited chatter of the village gossips keen not to miss a move of the uniforms. Matt was the focus of attention, but the Firmins gave his admirers short shrift as they elbowed their way up from the hard. Anne and the twins had already darted backwards and forwards a dozen times between the creek and their home kitchen, relaying what amounted to a running commentary to Mary Pullen of the events as they learned them, and so she was well prepared when Matt and Francis at last

put in an appearance, accompanied by the Firmins and a
few of the more dogged of their neighbors.

Mary Pullen was reminded of the night her husband
had been drowned, with all the comings and goings and
suppressed excitement. But now it was Beckett's death and
if, at Beckett's house, they were lamenting him (although
Charity had not yet come home), at the Pullen gathering
there were no tears being spilled on his behalf. The Firmins
were openly jubilant with the day's work. Francis, quietly
happy with his part in the day's events, sat yawning into his
tea mug and storing up this feeling of being accepted as a
smack hand, to him the ultimate honor, while Matt sat in
his father's chair nursing his bruises and trying to get used
to the idea that Beckett was dead.

"Aye, Mrs. Pullen," George said warmly, as she refilled
his mug. "That Beckett won't be harming this house again.
I shan't be flying my flag at half-mast for that old rogue,
I can tell you."

"What harm has Beckett done here," Mary Pullen asked
calmly, "save for trying to take Matt's prize today?"

"He stole your money off your husband's dead body and
half-killed Matt with a knife in Marchester," George said
bluntly. "Isn't that harm enough?"

Matt's mother stopped with the teapot in mid-air, staring
at George. "He *stole* that money? And—and Matt's arm—?"

Matt, meeting her shocked glance uncomfortably, said,
"It's finished now, George. We got the money back other
ways, and from under Beckett's nose, too, in the smack
race. And the arm mended soon enough."

"Your heart wouldn't have, and that's where it was meant
for," Clem put in.

"Well, he's lost his chance now," Matt said. He thought
suddenly of Beckett's face as he fell, when Beckett had

known, too, that he had lost, and he no longer felt much like rejoicing. Another couple of inches and he, too, might have been drifting with Beckett at the will of the tide, instead of easing mere bruises before his own hearth. His mother looked like a ghost.

"I never could fathom why he took such a sudden dislike to you that night in Marchester," George said. His blue eyes probed Matt's face. "Nor why he came home with a pair of black eyes and two front teeth missing."

There was a short silence. Matt knew that George deserved to know the whole tale, but it came reluctantly.

"When I went up to The Barge for the ale, I overheard him make a pact to see that *Juno* won the race. He knew I'd heard, too. He set three louts to follow me, but they'd been drinking." He grinned suddenly at his mother. "You see, I didn't lie to you. It *was* a drunken brawl."

Francis was looking as astonished as Mary Pullen.

"But why didn't you tell my father?"

"I had no need, did I? I knew if I got aboard the *Good Fortune* in the morning, Beckett wouldn't dare lose the race. And if he had, he knew I wouldn't hold my tongue then."

"My God!" Matt's simple courage flabbergasted George as completely as the recital of Beckett's deeds had shocked Matt's mother. "He lost out all ways at Marchester, then—and the smack race on top of that!" George's face lit up at the memory of Beckett's rage. "No wonder he looked so black! Why, I thought he had good enough reason to kill you just over the smack race, Matt, with the temper he carried—that and the fact you knew he'd got your father's money—I didn't know he'd tried to cheat Mr. Shelley into the bargain."

"And he was a good skipper," Matt couldn't help adding.

"No one could have got more out of the yacht than Beckett, not once he'd decided he'd got to win."

"Aye, well, she's in need of a new one now," Clem said.

Matt smiled at Francis. "You could apply, Francis. Late skipper of the *Reward*. Your father should have seen you handling the smack last night."

"I was on the mud when George met me," Francis said, flushing slightly.

"Ah, she was coming home nicely," George said. "There's not many lads'd pick it up so quick."

Francis flushed again, with pleasure this time.

Matt's mother shooed the round-eyed twins off to bed, and the Firmin brothers got up to go on home.

"Them revenue officers'll be scouring the county for the skipper of the old *Rose* tomorrow," George said as he set his empty mug down on the table.

"He'll be away by now," Clem said.

"Aye, back to Kent, where he comes from," said George.

"Where was he making for last night?" Matt asked.

"Marshfield, of course. That brandy was for Beckett to dispose of, didn't you know that? Beckett knew she'd gone astray, that's why he was out so sharp, while the tide was still making. And for you—of all people—to be salvaging his spirits! No wonder he tried to put you over the side!"

"I'd never heard of the *Rose*. I didn't know she was bound for Beckett," Matt said wonderingly. This last item of news left his muzzy head reeling with astonishment once more at the way fate had contrived to mix his path with Beckett's. He was as shaken as his mother had been a few minutes earlier, as shaken as George had been when he heard what had happened at Marchester.

"Aye, it was just as well, else you'd have given the *Rose* a miss, and things wouldn't have worked out so well for you. Beckett's death is the best thing that's happened in this place for a long time," George said firmly. "And I don't care who hears me say it. Good night to you, Mrs. Pullen. I'll see you tomorrow, Matt."

Matt nodded and tried to get out of his chair, but his limbs failed him. It was a long time, he felt, since he had seen his bed . . .

Francis lay watching the pale December sun washing the faded sills of the dormer window, reveling in the bliss of the feather mattress beneath him. He had almost forgotten what it was to lie awake, warm and comfortable, without the imminent prospect of a tide to catch, and an icy anchor chain to get aboard.

He yawned and stretched luxuriously. Beside him Matt lay sprawled, oblivious of the sun on his face. His salt-stiff thatch of hair glowed in the light. On his bare shoulder the bruises from his fall were spreading, blue and violet, to finger the scar that Francis could remember so vividly being patched by the competent Henry on the night of the regatta. Francis's mind went back to Matt threading the Firmins' smack along the Marchester waterside the first day they had met, to Matt appearing like a ghost over the *Good Fortune*'s counter on the day of the race, covered in grime and blood and sawdust, and as cool as if there were nothing amiss. No wonder Beckett had looked shaken! How his father was going to stare, Francis thought, when he heard the true story of that day!

As if Matt sensed Francis's thoughts dwelling on him, he opened his eyes. By force of habit he was instantly awake, but the pain of his first movement checked him with a surprised groan. Blinking at the sunlight, he cursed, then relaxed.

"It must be late," he said. "We'll have a day off on the strength of our salvage, eh? I'm too stiff to move."

Francis nodded and smiled. He got up, pulled on his clothes, and walked over to the window. The saltings, streaming and gleaming as the ebb left them, showed their rare, bleak beauty under the warmth of the winter sun. The seams of water which threaded them were silver in the light like veins of marble; the sea beyond flat and still and polished, as if it had never known a wreck or a drowning in all the centuries it had flowed ceaselessly up and down the estuary. Francis knew he would regret it when he was at home. Matt read his thoughts.

"You'll be going home for Christmas?" he said. "You've done what you wanted here, haven't you?"

"Yes."

Matt grinned. "Do you still think it's romantic—spratting?" he asked.

"It looks romantic enough out there now." Francis smiled back, avoiding the question.

"Aye, but what about last night?"

Francis shrugged at Matt's teasing, and Matt dropped his banter and said, "You've done well, though, as good as any regular hand. You've learned how to handle a smack and that's what you wanted, wasn't it? You've got guts to take it on. It's different for you, with your—your family and all. It's not hard for me. My father cuffed it into me before I was old enough to answer back, not that I'd have chosen any different. You used to think it was clever, didn't you? Now you can do it yourself—that proves it's simple enough. It'd take me more than a week or two to please your tutor, if we'd changed places!"

Francis did not argue. It was true that he had changed his concept of fishing for a livelihood these last few weeks, through living and working with Matt. The courage he had imagined, with which the fishermen faced their daily winter round, was in reality mere stoic indifference bred of familiarity. It was habit that sent them out on the first ebb into a November sea in the small hours of the morning, not courage. Matt had seen no heroism in riding out the night's gale to an anchor on the Buxey for the simple reason that there had been no heroism, only a professional appraisal of the conditions. Even his piloting of the big schooner through the Spitway had been, to put it barely, an exercise in judgment based on what all the local men knew of their territory, rather than the sensational magic Francis had seen at the time. The "romance," if any, lay in the nature of the sea itself and in the subtle and endless game it played with its combatants so that, for all their professionalism, the fishermen were never entirely safe. They lived to an old age only by permission of the sea. In their lives spent trying to outwit it, many were never granted that concession. It was this fact, Francis thought, rather than the mechanics of their trade, that had made him (and still did, in spite of his apprenticeship) think of them as a race apart, as "them," in fact. Just as he had the first day he had set eyes on Matt. He knew he would never come any closer to Matt than he was now, that he would never for all George's encouragement be any more of a smacksman than he was now, for he had neither the philosophy nor the endurance to face it day after day, tide after tide, year after year. The hours he had had *Reward* to himself, they had been his prize for a month's hard labor, and he would treasure them more dearly than any copperplate report of his tutor's in the years ahead. In future he would be satisfied with the *Good Fortune*, and with her comforts, too.

Matt lay back on the pillows, his eyes shut against the

sun. He could never remember feeling so completely at peace in his life before. The day Francis had come had changed his luck. Now within a month he had the two things he had begun to think would elude him all his life: his smack paid for and his fear of Beckett eliminated. He was completely his own master. Even if the *Good Fortune* went to Cowes and he never set eyes on Mr. Shelley again, his patronage meant nothing any longer. Matt knew he would thrive.

He knew, too, that his friendship with Francis had run its natural course. There were no regrets when the two boys shook hands that afternoon. Their ways were parting, but the warmth of the friendship would not fade. They had shared too much.

"You'll do well now," Francis said.

"Aye." That Francis would do well, too, was too obvious to waste breath in wishing.

Matt watched Francis walk away to join Henry at the Plough and Sail. It was raining, but Matt, watching the gulls wheeling about the gleaming mainmast of his own smack, *Reward*, saw only the shining brightness of her timbers. She was his own, and his living, and he wanted nothing else.